FLAWLESS

Haven 6

Gabrielle Evans

**EVERLASTING CLASSIC
MANLOVE**

Siren Publishing, Inc.
www.SirenPublishing.com

A SIREN PUBLISHING BOOK
IMPRINT: Everlasting Classic ManLove

FLAWLESS
Copyright © 2012 by Gabrielle Evans

ISBN: 978-1-62241-154-2

First Printing: July 2012

Cover design by Jinger Heaston
All art and logo copyright © 2012 by Siren Publishing, Inc.

PUBLISHER
Siren Publishing, Inc.
www.SirenPublishing.com

FLAWLESS

Haven 6

GABRIELLE EVANS
Copyright © 2012

Prologue

"Don't cheat," Lynk warned the little runt as he paused the game and went to answer the doorbell.

Wren resumed the game the minute he turned his back and giggled like a loon as he raced his car across the finish line. "I won!"

"Cheater!" Lynk called, laughing just as enthusiastically as Wren. The five-year-old pixie was about the cutest damn thing he'd ever seen in his life. He was young, so full of life, and everything was magical and exciting for him.

He'd never been around kids much before, didn't know the first thing about them, but it had taken approximately ten minutes for him to fall in love with Wren. He knew he wasn't as lost as his brother, Torren, though. Hopefully, with a little luck, Torren and his mate, Aslan, would be able to adopt Wren and give him a real home.

Still chuckling, he reached the front door and pulled it open. The laughter died in his throat, and he felt like he'd had the wind knocked out of him. The most stunning man he'd ever seen stood on the doorstep, his black hair cut short, just barely curling over his ears. Tall, much taller than Lynk, with muscles that looked to be sculpted from marble at the hands of an expert artist.

Smooth, creamy skin, with just the hint of sun, pulled tight over high cheekbones that highlighted gorgeous, mesmerizing, blue eyes. Lynk would have continued his leisurely exploration of the stranger, but he found himself lost in those cerulean eyes, unable to look away, move, or even breathe.

The stranger stared back at him, a low growl rumbling in his chest like rolling thunder. The heat of desire flashed in his eyes, turning them a darker shade of blue. Leaning forward slightly, his nostrils flared as he sniffed at Lynk's neck.

The sound of ripping fabric snapped Lynk out of his hypnosis, but not before he got a good look at the huge, russet-colored werewolf lunging for him. Not afraid for himself, but for Wren's safety, Lynk backpedalled, intent on slamming the door in the beast's face.

The wolf was faster, though, blocking the door with one hairy arm as he prowled closer, his gaze locked on the pulsing vein on Lynk's throat. His other arm shot out, looping around Lynk's waist and crushing him to the broad expanse of a chiseled chest.

Footsteps pounded behind him as the werewolf carried him farther into the house, and several loud gasps sounded. "What the fuck?" Raith yelled, snatching Wren up from the sofa and holding him protectively.

Enforcer Bannon Murphy looked on curiously, his eyes creasing at the corners while he studied the scene before him. "Kieran?"

The werewolf snapped his head up and snarled, tightening his grip until Lynk could barely breathe. Lynk struggled, trying to get away from the big brute, but he knew it was hopeless before he even began. The man had been much bigger than him before his shift, but now he was positively enormous.

"Kieran?" Galen stepped up beside Bannon and cocked his head to the side. "What has gotten into you? Put him down."

Kieran's nose began to nuzzle the side of Lynk's neck, and the rumble in his chest sped until it was almost a purr. His tongue snaked out, licking a slow, wet path that made Lynk's bones melt. He wasn't stupid. He knew exactly what was going on.

Kieran was his *Infinity*—literally the missing half of his torn soul. The bond was more intense than that of a normal fated pair, and Kieran's animal was reacting to that connection. It was all very logical and rational when put that way, but that didn't mean that Lynk enjoyed being handled like a piece of property.

"Put me down," he ordered.

Something whistled through the air a split second before it smacked against Kieran's nose. Galen was dancing around the werewolf, whacking him with a rolled up newspaper while spouting commands for him to release Lynk. Since that was exactly what he wanted, Lynk didn't argue, but anger welled up in him that Galen had struck his mate.

Torn between wanting to remain in Kieran's arms forever and beating the crap out of the Neanderthal, Lynk had a bad feeling it was going to be a recurring theme to the future of their relationship.

* * * *

"Put him down." Galen glared at him and stomped his foot. "Right now, Kieran. I mean it!" Something smacked against his nose again. "Now!"

Kieran gave the smaller man a fleeting glance and huffed out an annoyed breath. He hadn't been expecting to find his mate when he'd hopped in his truck and driven to Casper to talk to Torren. After the initial shock wore off, the attraction, the *need* was too intense to be ignored.

Nothing in life had prepared him for the aching desire to curl himself around the man in his arms and never, ever let go. He told himself he should set the guy on his feet and leave him be, but he couldn't. He was almost afraid, as though the world would cease to exist and his soul would bleed if he couldn't hold the man, touch him, smell him, taste him.

"Let me go, you stupid, overgrown, idiotic fur ball!" His mate struggled against him, but that only excited Kieran's wolf. Even when a solid kick connected with his knee, his brain barely registered the pain. Everything that he was revolved around this one man. Before he'd found his mate, he'd been wandering through life without purpose, waiting for something to bring meaning to an otherwise ordinary existence.

"What the hell is going on in here?" Torren stomped into the room, obviously in a temper, but he stumbled to a stop when his eyes landed on Kieran. Fine by him. He wanted everyone as far away from his mate as they could get.

"Umm, I'm going to guess that Lynk is Kieran's mate." Torren's lover, Aslan, tried to explain. His voice sounded a little shaky, but Kieran wasn't sure if it was from fear or amusement. "And he doesn't look like he'll be letting go any time soon."

His mate's name was Lynk. Kieran liked that. It fit his little man.

"Kieran Delaney, I'm going to call your sister."

Galen could do whatever the hell he wanted if he'd just go away and leave Kieran alone with his mate. Apparently the pipsqueak didn't like being ignored, though, because the rolled up newspaper arched through the air again. Galen missed him this time, though, striking Lynk on the shoulder instead.

The fury came swiftly, washing over him like a red haze until he was more animal than man, driven purely by instinct. Dropping Lynk to his feet and pushing the man behind him, he roared loud enough to vibrate every window in the house.

Bannon was just as fast, grabbing Galen around the waist and yanking him backward as he snarled right back at Kieran. There was a lot of yelling, shouting, and name-calling as Bannon and Torren advanced on him, but Kieran didn't care. What kind of man would he be if he didn't protect what was most important to him?

"Oh, for the love of Christmas." Lynk sounded irritated as he rounded Kieran and shoved him in the chest. The sound of his voice was enough to calm Kieran, but Lynk's amazing scent pushed him into a frenzy for an entirely different reason. "Would you knock it off already?" When he didn't respond to the words, Lynk grabbed a handful of fur on Kieran's chest and jerked him forward as he bared his throat in the ultimate act of surrender. "Just get it over with."

He didn't even pause to think about it before crushing Lynk close once more and sinking his canines into the soft, fragrant skin just above his collarbone. The bite went deep, but Kieran wanted to be sure that it remained, didn't fade, and would ache for days, letting Lynk know exactly who he belonged to.

Lynk bucked in his arms, arching against him so that his trapped erection rubbed against Kieran's hip, driving him crazy with lust. The smell of freshly spilled seed hit his nose, and Kieran's eyes rolled back in his head as he released Lynk's neck and licked lazily at his mating mark in satisfaction.

As he rubbed his head over Lynk's face, his neck, and every part of him he could reach, effectively marking the man with his scent, he felt his body shrinking, returning to his normal six-foot-four. When he could see in color again, his heart kicked hard against his sternum as he took in just how heartbreakingly beautiful Lynk really was.

His hands came up to cradle the masterpiece of Lynk's face, and he was sure he wore the smile of a lovesick idiot. Then hard knuckles connected with his jaw, sending him back a couple of steps to stare at Lynk in confusion. What the hell had just happened?

"Now go away." Lynk's tone was so frigid, Kieran was surprised that icicles didn't form on the light fixtures. Without giving Kieran a chance to retaliate, he spun on his heels and stormed out of the room as though the hounds of hell were chasing after him.

Kieran wasn't hurt or angry, though. Beneath that carefully constructed anger, he'd seen the fear in Lynk's eyes, the fear of a man who'd been hurt once too many. And come hell or high water, he'd prove to Lynk that he could be the one to take it all away.

Chapter One

Though he'd placed himself on the opposite side of the library, sitting in the same room with Kieran was pure torture. Lynk hadn't slept a wink since the man had claimed him in the living room of the house he shared with his brothers. Every time he even attempted to close his eyes, images of Kieran's stunning face appeared, his heart thrummed erratically, and his cock swelled in record time.

He'd managed to distance himself during the meeting and the gathering in the field that followed, always disappearing each time Kieran got too close. Did the werewolf know how sexy he'd looked prowling around the campfire? The glow of the flames had brushed his hair, his body, giving off the illusion that it was Kieran who lit up the clearing.

When shit hit the fan, Lynk had willingly pushed his personal issues aside to help in any way he could. He'd had the sense of being watched for most of the night and felt that something sinister hung on the air. So when Torren had ordered him to the main house to protect the residence within, he'd sprinted the entire way without question.

Now that everyone was safe, the threat had passed for the time being, and they had a plan to begin searching for the remainder of their missing brethren, the exhaustion was finally catching up to him. His magic was strong—though not as powerful as Torren's—but it was still draining to hold a protective spell for that long. Add that on top of his weary mind and sleep-deprived body, and Lynk thought he could probably sleep for the next week.

Unfortunately, he'd be leaving for Snake River as soon as the sun set the next evening. Torren had reason to believe that they'd find their brother, Thane, there, and Lynk had learned long ago that Torren was usually right. Not that he'd tell the arrogant bastard that, but still, he knew.

Curled up in one of the armchairs in the back corner of the room, he watched Wren wrap his arms around Torren's neck and squeeze him tightly. "I love you, Daddy."

The words were quiet, just barely reaching Lynk. It caused a lump to form in his throat, and his eyes stung when he saw the emotions playing across Torren's face. Despite his many faults, Torren deserved to be happy, to have someone love him unconditionally. Lynk had no doubts that Torren would be an amazing father.

He must have nodded off after that, because when he came to again, people were murmuring their good-byes and trickling out of the library. Lynk couldn't make his tired limbs move to haul him up from his resting place, though. His eyelids began to droop again, his head feeling much too heavy for him to lift it.

Jerking awake when he felt strong arms slide under him and lift him out of the chair, he started to protest, but Kieran was already sitting, settling Lynk securely in his lap. Gods, he was so warm. And Lynk was weak. He knew he needed to get up and walk away, but how could he when it was exactly where he'd wanted to be all night?

"Hush now," Kieran whispered to him, stroking Lynk's shoulder-length hair, digging his fingers in to massage the back of his scalp. "Just rest, sugar. I've got you."

"I shouldn't want this."

Kieran didn't argue with him, didn't say anything as he continued petting him, soothing him in a way he hadn't felt in such a long time. His brain began to shut down, giving him the first measure of peace he'd had in weeks. His eyelids wouldn't stay open, succumbing to gravity and plunging him into darkness.

His mate.

His *Infinity*.

The missing half of his soul that had been ripped from the core of his being and given a home in the one person that would forever be by his side to understand him, defend him, cherish him...love him.

Lynk's beginning and end.

Kieran was his answer, but what was the question? And if Kieran was the question, what could possibly be the answer?

The endless riddles continued churning, rolling, swirling inside his brain, over and over until he thought he'd go mad from them. Kieran was the light to his darkness, given to Lynk to balance his self-destructive behavior. How could he in good conscience allow the coldness within him to seep over and pollute his mate?

Kieran Delaney was pure. His heart was kind, warm, the place a person would want to take up residence and spend the rest of their days. Being with Lynk would change him, though. It would change him in ways that Lynk didn't want to think about.

"I can't." He couldn't do it. He couldn't tarnish Kieran that way, wouldn't cloud his soul with bone-numbing darkness. So he struggled, tried to get away. He pushed at Kieran's chest, heaved his shoulders, twisted one way and then the other.

Kieran held him tight as he thrashed about, not giving in to Lynk's panic. Rough, callused fingers gripped his chin, pushing his head back on his shoulders. "Quiet," Kieran commanded, his voice soft but firm, holding a velvet steel that made Lynk shiver from the base of his skull clear down to his toes.

Did Kieran see his trembling muscles? Did he notice how Lynk had calmed at once? Was he disgusted with Lynk's reaction to him? Whatever was going on inside his mind, his face gave nothing away.

"When is the last time you slept?"

"The night before last," Lynk answered automatically.

Kieran traced under Lynk's eyes with his fingertips. "When is the last time you *really* slept? I don't mean closed your eyes for a couple of hours, but really, really slept."

Lynk bit the inside of his cheek and shook his head. He understood the question, but he honestly couldn't remember the last time he'd had a decent night's sleep. This close to Kieran, he couldn't think of anything but the heat pouring off of the man's body, the hard muscles beneath his soft shirt, and how incredible he smelled.

"That's what I thought." Kieran's voice was low, husky, and dripping with arousal. He shifted in his seat, and Lynk felt the evidence of that desire pressed against his ass.

His own cock hardened in response, swelling to strain against his zipper. When Kieran's hand landed on his upper thigh and squeezed, Lynk thought he'd come right there in his jeans. The breathless moan that puffed through his lips embarrassed him, but he couldn't stop it.

"Come on." Kieran stood, still cradling Lynk in his arms as he stomped across the room and out into the hallway.

"Where are we going?"

"I'm going to put you in my bed, and you're going to sleep."

Lynk started to struggle. As much as he'd love to be in Kieran's bed, it was a terrible idea. "No. I'll stay here. There has to be a spare room that I can use."

"I imagine there is, but I said you're coming with me."

The authority in his voice went straight to Lynk's cock. His erection jerked, leaking pre-cum from the slit until he could see the small stain spreading across the front of his pants. Riding on the tail end of that lust was an overwhelming anxiety, though. Did Kieran know his secret? Could he see just by looking at him?

"Kieran, put me down." He tried to be firm, to speak with conviction, but even to his own ears, he could hear the underlying plea. Maybe he should just haul off and punch his mate again. That had seemed to do the trick the last time—except that he'd felt sick about it from the moment it had happened.

He'd been given a gift, and not only had he forsaken it, turned it away, but he'd gone as far as to abuse it. What the fuck was wrong with him?

* * * *

Kieran could feel the way Lynk trembled in his arms, but he didn't think it was from fear. There was some anxiety there. Kieran could feel it as well as scent a slight trace of it on the air. Still, he didn't think Lynk was afraid of him, but more that the man was nervous around him. He'd never say it out loud, but he kind of liked knowing that Lynk wasn't as unaffected as he pretended to be.

Looking at Torren and Raith, anyone would expect Lynk to be just as big, just as brawny. They'd be sorely disappointed. While he wasn't much larger than Aslan or any of the other mates in the house, Kieran could feel the hard muscles bunching under his palms, knew if he got his mate naked, those muscles would be sculpted and defined.

None of that mattered to him, though. The fact that Lynk was gorgeous from the tips of his shiny black hair to his smaller than average feet was just icing on the cake. The beauty he sought lurked on the inside. Beneath the veneer of cool indifference, there was a kind, giving soul just searching for someone to nurture it and bring it to the surface.

Kieran knew he was more than up for the job.

"Kieran, put me down."

It was cute the way his mate argued with him, but it so wasn't happening. "Have you ever just let someone take care of you?"

Nope. He could see the confusion written all over Lynk's face.

"I can take care of myself."

"You're adorable when you pout." Kieran chuckled at the scowl on Lynk's plump lips. "I have no doubt that you can do anything you put your mind to, but that's not the point. Everyone needs to be pampered sometimes."

Finally settling Lynk on his feet, Kieran checked to make sure the foyer was clear of any sun-allergic vampires and punched in the access code so that the steel plates covering the door slid away.

Taking Lynk's wrist, he pulled him out into the morning sun, closed the door behind them, and waited until he heard the door covering grind back into place.

"Where do you live?"

Smiling to himself, Kieran held his mate's hand as he led him along the dirt path that would take them to the cabin he shared with his brothers. "It's not far. Just around that curve in the road. Raina and Teegan used to share the cabin with us, but they moved up to the main house after the pups were kidnapped. Once things settle down, they'll move to one of the cabins across the lake."

He just kept talking, keeping his voice low and soothing, offering idle chit-chat in hopes that it would calm some of Lynk's nervousness. The grip on his hand remained steady, unflinching, so he took that as a good sign.

"What do people think is going on here?" Lynk waved his hand around vaguely. "I mean, this place is huge. It's not like you can hide it from the people in town, even if it is way out here in the sticks."

"Well, I'd guess the humans probably think we're some kind of cult or commune. Most of the surrounding towns are occupied by paranormals, though, so it's not really an issue. They know what we are, and for the most part, they just leave us to it."

He'd never really speculated on what the humans believed of their little community, but now, the thought made him chuckle. No doubt they had all sorts of gruesome ideas about what went on inside the iron gates of Haven.

"I'm sorry that I hit you." The words were said so quietly, Kieran almost thought he imagined them until Lynk spoke again. "I had no right to do that. My only excuse is that I panicked and reacted badly."

Kieran didn't respond, but he squeezed the hand in his with reassurance. He hadn't been angry about Lynk's right hook to his jaw. A little dazed perhaps, a lot confused, but anger had never factored into the equation. Lynk's apology was sincere, but something in the way he said it didn't sit right with Kieran.

From the moment Kieran had lifted him out of that chair in the library, Lynk had said a number of things that didn't make sense to him. He hadn't said he didn't want Kieran to hold him, he'd said he "shouldn't" want it.

It also didn't escape his notice the way Lynk practically quivered when Kieran used his "alpha" voice. Nor did he miss how his mate had stilled at once when Kieran had ordered it. He'd only wanted to prevent Lynk from hurting himself, but he couldn't deny the man's reaction had sent a jolt straight to his aching cock. He just didn't understand what any of it meant.

"Did I say something wrong?"

Studying Lynk's bent head, his downcast eyes, and the way his shoulders rounded as though drawing in on himself, Kieran felt the first threads of uncertainty. There was obviously something he was missing, something that Lynk needed from him but was afraid to ask for. Lynk wasn't pack, shouldn't respond the way he did to Kieran's commands. Yet, he was more…obedient than any of Kieran's siblings.

Obedience. What an odd word for him to use for a human being, but it was the only thing he could think to describe Lynk's behavior. Kieran was used to taking control and being in charge. While he knew from talking to Torren that Lynk had some wicked powerful magic, the man was so unassuming that no one would ever realize it.

Lynk was beginning to shake again, his hand wobbling in Kieran's grasp. He was obviously uncomfortable with Kieran's lack of communication.

Not knowing how else to comfort the man, Kieran scooped him up in his arms, nuzzled the side of his neck, and made a sound somewhere between a growl and purr. Lynk calmed at once, breathing out a contented sigh as he curled closer and fisted his hands in Kieran's shirt.

It was a dirty trick, but it worked, and Kieran would take whatever advantage he could get until he figured out what the hell was going on with his very peculiar mate.

Chapter Two

Stepping up on the front porch of the large cabin, Lynk had a momentary sense of panic when all three of Kieran's brothers stepped outside and took up ranks, barricading the entrance to their home. Sweet hell, were they putting steroids in the water? Everyone he'd met apart from Aslan and his friends was big enough to double as the side of a barn. Even Torren and Raith seemed better suited to the wrestling ring than some backwoods town in Wyoming.

A steady hand landed on his lower back and rubbed in soothing circles. "Guys, this is my mate, Lynk Braddock. Lynk, these idiots are my brothers, Parker, Jericho, and Elijah, but we call him Eli."

"They don't look very happy to see me," he commented, moving a little closer to Kieran's side.

"They're not big fans of Torren's, so you're kind of getting the evil eye by association. They won't hurt you, though." Kieran pushed him forward a step, and surprisingly, the brothers parted to allow them entrance into the house.

"Kieran, if they don't want me here maybe I should just go back up to the main house."

"Nah, it's cool," one of the men answered. Lynk knew their names. He just didn't know which one was which. "I'm Parker, and your brother is an egotistical fuckhead. You seem okay, but I'll reserve judgment."

"Parker!" Kieran barked. "Go be stupid somewhere else."

"I'm Jericho." He appeared to be the youngest of the group. "My sister would probably lop my balls off if I was rude to you, so if you talk to her, tell her that I was minding my manners." He held his hand out, which Lynk took hesitantly.

"Don't mind these idiots." The last one, who had to be Eli, nudged Jericho out of the way and snatched Lynk's hand, giving it a firm squeeze before releasing it. "We're happy to have you here. As for you being mated to Kieran, well, good luck with that. He's a bigger asshole than your brother."

Lynk frowned down at the floor. He didn't think the men were being fair at all. Kieran didn't seem like an asshole. Granted, he didn't know the man very well, though. Torren could be a bit arrogant and kind of uptight, but they were talking about him like he was Attila the Hun or something.

"Torren is a good man with a big heart. I know he can come off as conceited, but that's mostly to hide all of his insecurities. He would do anything in his power to help any of you."

Parker just grunted, seemingly unconvinced. Eli and Jericho stared at Lynk like he was speaking another language. Kieran, however, was grinning from ear to ear as he wrapped an arm around Lynk's waist and bent to nuzzle the back of his neck. He did that a lot, but Lynk wasn't going to complain since he loved it.

"I've been trying to tell them the same thing for months. You explained so much better than I could, though. Don't ever be scared to defend the people you care about, baby. I got your back."

Well, in that case…

"And Kieran isn't an asshole, either. He's kind, warm, brave, and loyal. He's also your alpha, and you should have more respect." Lynk was trembling violently by the time he'd finished speaking, but Kieran said he should protect and defend the people he cared about. He might not know much about his mate yet, but he already cared too much to let someone slander the man he knew Kieran to be.

"He's also our brother," Jericho said with a snort. "We're just fucking around with him. Don't you give your brothers shit? That's all it is. We're only trying to make sure that his head doesn't swell so big that he can't fit through the doorway."

"Okay, knock it off. Patrol duty starts in thirty minutes. You guys are going to have to go without me. Be sure to check on the new Moonlighters and see how they're settling in. Also, ask the alpha, Xander, if there is anything he needs. Varik and Demos are headed to Snake River tonight along with Lynk..." He trailed off, a frown tugging at the corners of his lips.

"And you want to go with them," Eli surmised. "Don't worry about it, man. We've got shit covered here. You'll be a wreck wondering about Lynk and no use around here anyway."

"Thanks, pup." Kieran clapped his brother on the shoulder. "I knew I could count on you guys." Then he took Lynk's hand and gave it a small tug. "Time to get you settled. Would you like a shower first?"

A hot shower sounded like heaven. "Please," he practically moaned.

Everyone chuckled, and Kieran bent and kissed him on the forehead. "None of our clothes will fit, but I'll see if I can find something that won't completely swallow you." He led Lynk through what he assumed was Kieran's bedroom and pointed into the bathroom. "Everything you need is in there. I'll leave some clothes on the bed and give you some privacy."

After nodding his understanding, Lynk closed the bathroom door quietly but left it unlocked. Part of him hoped that Kieran would join him in the shower. That part was likely connected to his dick, which had been hard and throbbing since Kieran had first lifted him into his arms back at the mansion.

The bigger, rational part of his brain was demanding to know what the hell he was doing there in the first place. Nothing good could come from his pairing with Kieran.

Torren hadn't remembered any of his previous lives with Aslan until after he'd claimed his mate. Lynk didn't have that luxury. He remembered every minute of each of his three lives in vivid detail. Though Kieran wouldn't understand, the kindest thing he could do for his new mate was run in the opposite direction and never look back.

Even as he contemplated it, Kieran's beautiful blue eyes invaded his mind, staring straight into him as though he could see his soul. Sighing in defeat, and knowing he'd regret it later, Lynk shook his head and stepped into the shower.

* * * *

"You sure about this guy, Kieran?"

"Yes," Kieran answered shortly as he dug through his dresser, searching for something Lynk could wear. He came up with a pair of sweats that at least had a drawstring and a faded blue T-shirt. Not great, but it would have to do.

"Look, I know he's your mate and all, but he's also a Braddock." Parker was like a dog with a fucking bone. He wasn't going to let this thing go until either Lynk proved himself or Kieran put him in his place.

Not wanting to drag Lynk into the middle of it when he already seemed so on edge, Kieran figured he was going to have to nip this one in the bud himself. Dropping the clothes on the bed, he spun Parker around by his shoulder and shoved him toward the door, not wanting Lynk to overhear their conversation. Besides, he only wanted to say it once.

Gathering everyone in the living room, he motioned for them all to sit while he stood in the center of the room and crossed his arms over his chest. "Lynk is my mate. I've already claimed him. He is not—and I repeat *not*—Torren, so whatever beef you have with his brother, you do not take it out on Lynk. If anyone has a problem with him being here, then spit it out now."

"We don't know anything about this guy. How do we know he didn't bewitch you or something?"

Kieran stared at Parker in disbelief. "What is your issue with witches? I really can't believe you just fucking said that to me. If anything, he doesn't want to be here. Hell, he decked me in the jaw after I claimed him. Does that sound like someone who would spell me into wanting him?"

Parker had the good sense to look ashamed of himself as he sucked his bottom lip between his teeth and averted his eyes. "No, I guess not." Then his eyes lit up and a slow smile spread across his face. "He really punched you?"

"The little shit has a mean right hook." Kieran rubbed at his jaw and laughed. "So, I would suggest not pissing him off."

"He doesn't seem like he'd have it in him," Jericho commented. "I mean, he's, well, he acts kind of shy and guarded. I thought he was going to vibrate right out of his skin when he was telling us all off for talking shit about his brother, like he was afraid to stand up to us."

Yeah, Kieran didn't get it, either. There would be plenty of time for him to learn the inner workings of his mate, though. Probably. Hopefully. "So, we're all cool? I don't want to do it, but if your bullshit is going to be an ongoing thing, then I'll take Lynk and go back to The Council house in Casper. Are we clear?"

"I got no problem with the guy." Eli shrugged, offered him a lopsided smile, and sauntered off into the kitchen.

"He likes you, so I have concerns about his sanity, but otherwise, I think he's all right." Jericho pushed up from the armchair and punched Kieran in the arm. "Congrats, bro."

That only left Parker. The man sat forward on the sofa and linked his fingers together between his knees. "You really care about him? Already? After one day?"

"Yes." He couldn't explain it, blamed a lot of it on the mating bond, but it was there nonetheless. "He's important to me."

Parker stared down at his clasped hands and nodded slowly before rising to his feet and offering Kieran his hand. "Then I'll figure it out.

He won't get any more shit from me. I'm happy for you, Kieran. I'm glad you found your mate."

Clasping his brother's hand, Kieran jerked him into a one-armed hug. "Thank you. It means a lot, Parker."

Obviously uncomfortable with Kieran's display of emotion, Parker released him with a grunt and hightailed it to the kitchen. "He'll come around," Jericho offered before following after him, leaving Kieran standing alone in the middle of the living room.

Kieran didn't know what Parker's problem was or why he had such an adverse reaction to all things Braddock, but he intended to find out. He was almost to the kitchen when he heard the shower shut off down the hall. Pausing midstep, he was torn between confronting Parker and sprinting straight to his room and Lynk.

He must have stood there longer than he realized, because the decision was suddenly taken out of his hands when Lynk stepped through the door and turned to face him. His raven hair was all damp and sleek, brushing against the tops of his shoulders and curling just a little at the ends.

The dark blue sweatpants were rolled several times at the bottom, and, Kieran imagined, a few times at the waist. The T-shirt he'd left out was one of his favorite, well worn and soft from so many washings. It was a little loose on Kieran, but it completely devoured Lynk. The sleeves alone fell to his elbows, while the hem settled around midthigh.

Deciding he liked his balls right where they were, Kieran didn't say a word about how hard his dick was at the sight of Lynk in his clothes and knowing that the man was completely smothered in his scent. He also wouldn't mention that was why he'd suggested the shower and change of clothes, either.

He'd detected several different scents on Lynk—some he knew and some he didn't. None of them had been Kieran's, though, and that just wouldn't do. While he didn't comment on his thoughts, he couldn't stop the satisfied grin.

"You look a little too pleased," Lynk observed, giving Kieran a shy smile in return.

"No such thing." He stalked down the hallway, not slowing until he had his arms around his mate, lifting him up so he could capture that sweet, pouty mouth. Part of his brain screamed that he was moving too fast, that he should back off until Lynk was more comfortable with him, but he'd been dying for a taste since he'd first set eyes on the witch.

Lynk moaned breathily, his arms slipping around Kieran's neck and holding on tight. Sliding his tongue back and forth along the seam of Lynk's closed lips, Kieran growled while his wolf howled in approval. "Open for me," he demanded, barely recognizing his own voice.

"Oh, gods," Lynk breathed, his lips parting to allow Kieran entrance.

Taking full advantage, Kieran plunged inside, sweeping his tongue around his mate's mouth, pillaging the moist depths. Lights danced behind his closed eyelids, electricity zinged through his body, and he thought he might actually swoon when his dick swelled to the point of pain and pounded against his zipper.

Lynk remained passive, allowing him to dominate the kiss, but his hips rocked, grinding his erection over Kieran's abs as the most delicious whimpers escaped him, pouring into Kieran's open mouth. Their tongues met, twined, swirled together in a slippery dance. Then Lynk's fingers found their way into Kieran's short hair, tangling and pulling as though desperate to have him closer.

Keeping one hand on Lynk's firm ass to hold him up, Kieran slid his other beneath the hem of his mate's shirt, pushing it up so that he could get to the bare flesh beneath. Just as he'd imagined, Lynk's skin was soft and so damn warm, stretched tight over tense, quivering, and tightly packed muscles.

Stumbling backward into his room, he kicked the door closed and turned to drop Lynk to the mattress, following him down and prowling up his body. Feeling as though he was burning from the inside out, he stripped his shirt over his head then turned his attention to Lynk's, practically shredding it in his need to get his man naked.

A very unmanly whimper bubbled up in his throat when he finally got a good look at Lynk's nude torso. Sinewy shoulders, broad pectorals, and corrugated abdominals—the man was a walking advertisement for sex, only travel-sized. The too-big sweatpants slid down his narrow waist, showing off his hip bones where they protruded slightly to form the triangular valley of his groin.

The prize Kieran sought, however, was currently tenting the front of the soft cotton, rising up to greet him like a long lost friend. Even through the baggy pants, the outline of Lynk's cock was enough to make his mouth water and his nostrils flare.

As much as he'd love to slip a hand inside Lynk's waistband and wrap it around the turgid flesh, the choice wasn't his. Lynk was breathing hard, his body responding in all the right ways, but his eyes, which always seemed to know more than he was telling, were too wide, too startled.

Reeling in his desire, Kieran rolled to the side and propped himself up on one elbow while he smoothed his palm over Lynk's stomach, trying to calm rather than arouse. "If I promise to behave myself, will you let me sleep beside you while you rest?"

Lynk looked a little surprised, but didn't comment for a long time while he studied Kieran, perhaps searching for the truth in his eyes. Kieran kept his expression neutral and gave nothing away. Whatever decision was made, he wouldn't sway his mate one way or another.

Then just when he thought Lynk wasn't going to answer him, a soft, tentative smile curled the corners of his lips, and his head tilted almost imperceptibly. "I'd like that."

Resisting the urge to whoop like a little boy on Christmas morning, Kieran scooted up the bed and under the blankets, holding back a corner for Lynk to cuddle in beside him. To his utter delight, Lynk snuggled right up to his chest, sighed softly, and closed his eyes.

Ignoring his persistent erection, Kieran wound both arms around Lynk, pulled him closer, and kissed the top of his head. "Thank you."

"No," Lynk whispered. "Thank you."

Kieran didn't know what the gratitude was for, but he wasn't going to question it right then. For the first time in his life, he felt like everything was right in the world and he was exactly where he was supposed to be.

Chapter Three

It wasn't easy getting to sleep with his body so hyperaware of his mate's proximity. While he'd enjoyed everything Kieran had done to him, right down to his aggressive, take-charge attitude, Lynk had been hard-pressed to control the anxiety that swarmed him. If they had any chance at a future together, he was going to have to come clean with the werewolf. Wrapped up in Kieran's arms, feeling safe and cherished like he'd never felt before, it was hard to worry about those kinds of things, though.

He must have eventually drifted off to sleep, because the next thing he knew, Kieran was trailing wet kisses down the back of his neck to wake him up. "You have to meet Varik and Demos in about an hour," he mumbled, not pausing in his attempt to drive Lynk out of his mind.

Why on earth would he want to go meet a couple of vampires who would take him to see even more vampires when he had everything he wanted right there in bed with him? Oh, right, because Torren had reason to believe that their brother, Thane, resided somewhere within the walls of the Snake River Coven.

Finding their brothers was top priority, not to mention that Lynk missed having his family close. He wasn't stupid or naïve, however. Finding Thane in Snake River was going to incite a war he didn't know if he was ready to fight. If the coven was holding Thane prisoner, that meant they'd also held Torren's mate, Aslan, as a slave at some point.

In the best of circumstances, Torren wouldn't let something like that slide. Factor in Aslan, the man he loved more than anyone on earth, and it was just asking for a battle of epic proportions. Then there was the little detail about Snake River being the former home and coven of not only Stavion, but all of his Enforcers as well.

While he hoped to find Thane quickly and mostly unharmed, if they found him with that particular coven, all hell was going to break loose.

"Hey, what's wrong?" Kieran's hand slid up Lynk's chest and stroked him in slow circles. "Everything is going to be okay, Lynk. I promise."

"You can't promise that. Do you realize that we're screwed either way you slice this? If we find Thane, then Torren is going to want to wipe out the entire coven, not just because of what they've done to our brother, but because of what happened to Aslan. If we don't find Thane, we've still made an enemy for bringing Snake River under suspicion. There is no way to win this one."

"If they have your brother, they need to be brought to justice, baby. What I've learned since I've been here is that these kinds of things don't just happen in twos and threes. There is no telling how many people they are holding or have bought, sold, or traded in the past. They have to be stopped before anyone else gets hurt. In my book, that's a win."

"You don't think Stavion will fight against it? That is his old coven." Lynk rolled until he could face his mate, very interested in what Kieran had to say on the matter. He loved listening to the man talk. Kieran was intelligent, but he didn't use fancy words or act like he was better than anyone. He simply told it like it was.

"Honestly, no. Jory came from a situation like Aslan's, but even worse. There is not a single thing in this world that is more important to Stavion than his mate—not Haven, not his old coven, *nothing*. And that's exactly how it should be."

Lynk wondered about the eagle-shifters who had held him and the faerie, Camdin, in that abandoned slaughterhouse. "The shifters from Pennsylvania—they're not in the holding cells at the house in

Casper." Okay, so not a question, but he wasn't even sure what he wanted to know, let alone how to ask it.

"No, they're not." Kieran growled, and for the first time, it was frightening rather than sexy. "They're here in Haven, in the basement cells at the main house. They want to find out who the witches are that they're working with before The Council hands down its sentence."

After letting that digest for a few seconds, Lynk dipped his head in understanding and rolled out of bed. The instant he was on his feet, so were his sweatpants, slipping off his hips and pooling on the carpet around his ankles.

"Well, good morning to you as well," Kieran teased him, but Lynk didn't miss the fire in his eyes or the way his tongue darted out to lick his lips.

Neither did a thing to cool the ardor he felt thrumming through his body. Just by being so close to his mate, his cock was already hard and weeping. Now that Kieran was looking at him like he wanted to eat him, Lynk's dick jerked and his balls squeezed tight to his body, practically begging for attention.

Emotionally, he wasn't sure how he felt about Kieran. His soul bond with the man kept getting in the way and muddling everything. Carnally, however, he'd never wanted anyone more. Possessive, commanding, confident—Kieran was all the things he liked in a man rolled up in one incredibly tantalizing package.

"We need to get you some clothes that will fit," Kieran said, shaking himself and looking away from Lynk's groin.

Grabbing the waistband of his sweats, Lynk jerked them back up his hips and held them cinched together with both hands. "All of my things are in Casper." He didn't have much, just a couple pairs of jeans and a handful of T-shirts, but there hadn't been a lot of time for things like shopping since he'd been rescued from the eagle-shifters.

"Where did you come from? I mean, before you were kidnapped, where did you live? Do you have things that we need to have sent here?"

"No!" Lynk bit his lip and blushed clear to the tips of his ears. "I…I, umm, everything I have is in Casper." It wasn't technically a lie. None of the things in that big house on Lake Erie belonged to him.

"We have a cache of extra clothes, shoes, and shit like that over in the dorms." Kieran rolled out of bed and plodded to the bathroom, not even looking at Lynk. "We never know when people will show up with nothing more than the clothes on their backs—and sometimes not even that much. You can borrow what you need."

Lynk's heart beat a little faster at the detached tone in his mate's voice. He wasn't exactly sure what he'd done, or what had happened, but it was obvious that Kieran was less than happy with him. Taking a deep breath to gather his courage, he shuffled into the bathroom, pausing just inside the doorway.

The shower was already running, beating against the porcelain bottom of the tub while Kieran stripped out of his clothes, his back to Lynk the entire time. With his heightened senses, he had to know Lynk was there, yet he made no show of acknowledgement.

"Did I do something to make you angry?"

"No." Stepping into the shower, Kieran closed the door with enough force to rattle the glass. "Just wait in the living room, and I'll take you over to the dorms when I'm finished."

Indecision swarmed him. Should he do as he'd been told and leave Kieran to himself? Or should he make a bold move, step into that shower, and demand to know what was going on? It wasn't in his nature to be aggressive or forward, but he hated the cramp in his stomach from the thought that Kieran could be unhappy with him for any reason.

Acting on instinct, he dropped his sweats, stepped out of them, and slid the door back to reveal Kieran's wet, tanned, naked backside.

The werewolf tensed, but said nothing to discourage him, so Lynk stepped into the shower, closed the door, and waited. When Kieran still wouldn't turn and look at him, Lynk thought he was going to throw up.

Instead, he grabbed the liquid soap from the shelf, poured a generous amount into his palm, and warmed it before lathering it over Kieran's back. Ignoring everything else, he focused on the soft skin and tight muscles beneath his palms, scrubbing his mate's shoulders, back, hips, and his gloriously firm ass.

Grabbing more soap, he once again let it warm in his hands before crouching down to wash each of Kieran's legs, starting with his massive thighs and moving down to his surprisingly slender ankles. Then he tugged on his mate's wrist, pleased when Kieran turned to face him, but feeling a slight pang when he kept his eyes closed.

Repeating the routine, Lynk stroked and cleaned Kieran's shoulders, chest, abs, down each thigh, and quickly and clinically made a pass over his hard cock and tight sac. "I can't reach your hair," he whispered.

Without a word or opening his eyes, Kieran knelt in the tub, sitting back on his heels and resting his hands in his lap. It hurt to see him like that, but Lynk knocked away the guilt that threatened to undo him and began working the shampoo through Kieran's short hair, taking the time to massage his scalp and temples.

"Lean your head back, please."

Kieran did as asked, and Lynk quickly rinsed the suds away, lingering just a little longer than necessary because he couldn't bring himself to release the man just yet. When he finally made himself step away, he was halted by Kieran's hands on his hips.

"Be still," Kieran commanded, his voice deep and raspy. Lynk's body obeyed without conscious decision on his part.

Kieran nuzzled against his stomach, rubbing his cheek over the jumping muscles before placing a soft kiss on Lynk's belly button. His fingers clenched and relaxed, kneading the flesh on Lynk's hips and dragging him closer. After skimming his nose up Lynk's chest, inhaling deeply the entire way, Kieran followed the trail back down, laving wet, open-mouth kisses over his slick skin.

"You will not lie to me." It wasn't a request. There was a hard, demanding undercurrent to his tone that made Lynk shiver right down to his curling toes. "Do you understand?"

"Yes, sir."

The words burst through his lips, barely louder than a breath, but Kieran growled his approval before nipping at Lynk's hip. "You will not hide from me."

"No, sir."

Kieran growled again, louder this time, and Lynk almost came right where he was standing. "Now, tell me, Lynk, do you want me to stop?" His tongue lapped at the tip of Lynk's cock and swirled around the engorged crown.

"No." He couldn't take his eyes off of those plump lips as they stretched wide around his throbbing shaft. His knees trembled, threatening to buckle with every slide of Kieran's tongue along the underside of his length.

Kieran gave him a couple of good strokes with his mouth before popping off and sitting back on his heels again. "What do you want, Lynk?"

The inquiry confused him. He'd never been asked that question and wasn't sure how to respond. He definitely wanted Kieran to keep sucking his cock, but he couldn't ask for that. Kieran shouldn't have been on his knees in the first place.

Shame and guilt slammed into him, making his throat constrict painfully. His thoughts raced out of control, chasing each other around his brain as he fought to find a way to fix this. "I want to suck your cock, sir."

Kieran's long fingers surrounded his shaft and squeezed. "Are you sure about that, sugar?"

"Yes, sir." Lynk bobbed his head quickly even as he struggled to remain still and not thrust into Kieran's tight grasp.

"What if I don't want that?"

Well, shit. "Whatever would please you, sir. Whatever you want."

He felt more than heard Kieran's sigh, but he didn't understand it. He didn't have long to contemplate what it meant, either. Those talented fingers squeezed him harder, jerking his cock from base to tip with skilled movements.

"I want you to come for me, Lynk." Kieran twisted his wrist, rubbing the side of his forefinger along the bundle of nerves just under the crown. "Now."

Like a bomb just waiting for detonation, Lynk groaned quietly as his orgasm plowed into him, sending reams of seed spurting from his slit. When his mate's mouth closed over the head of his cock and sucked hard, demanding Lynk give him everything, he thought he'd die from the intense pleasure.

His climax seemed to go on forever, and when he drifted down from his euphoric high, he found himself cradled in Kieran's lap. He'd given the man exactly what he'd asked for, so why did he feel like he'd failed in some way? "I'm sorry."

"I don't want to hear those words again. Are we clear?"

Feeling more confused and wrung out than he could ever remember, Lynk bobbed his head in acquiescence. "Yes, sir."

"Get clean and dressed." Kieran lifted him out of his lap and stood with his hand on the glass door. "I need to pack before I take you to the dorms."

"Pack?" Kieran was going somewhere?

"You didn't think I was going to let you go off to Snake River alone, did you?"

"Demos and Varik will be with me," Lynk responded automatically.

Kieran just smirked at him before stepping out of the shower. "Yes, but they aren't me."

No, they definitely weren't. As far as Lynk was concerned, there wasn't another person on earth like Kieran. "Can I ask why you're coming with us?"

"You can." Lynk heard the bathroom door open as he reached for the shampoo, and he paused to wait for Kieran's response. "Doesn't mean I'll answer." Then the door closed with a quiet snick, effectively ending the conversation.

Chapter Four

After raiding the dorm's supplies for clothes and shoes for Lynk, Kieran led his mate through the moonlight to the main house to meet with the vampire Enforcers. It wasn't that he didn't trust Demos and Varik to keep Lynk safe, but neither of them had a personal interest in the witch's well-being—not like Kieran did.

Besides, he didn't like the idea of Lynk going into a possibly volatile situation where his two main protectors were hindered by the sunlight. Just because they were going to a vampire coven didn't mean there wouldn't be other threats to Lynk in the light of day.

Stepping in through the front door, they were immediately greeted by Demos, Varik, and the two alphas of the new packs that had settled into Haven. Kieran wasn't sure how he felt about a bunch of Moonlighters hanging around the place. He'd grown up hearing the legends surrounding the white-pelted breed, been told repeatedly how they could drive anyone to insanity within minutes just by shifting in front of them.

Since being in Haven, he'd also been told how it was all a bunch of horse hockey. It wasn't easy to wipe away a lifetime of teachings, though. Now that he had Lynk to worry about, he wasn't going to follow blindly without someone offering him some proof. According to Stavion, the breed only posed a threat when they were shifted *and* only to the person at which their rage was directed. Maybe so, but he was still reserving judgment.

The men made no move to approach them, which was already winning them points in Kieran's book. "I'm Kieran Delaney, and this is my mate, Lynk Braddock. Welcome to Haven." He dropped his backpack to the floor and held his hand out to the man closest to him, further impressed when the shifter shook it firmly, but made no move to try to intimidate him with his larger size.

"Xander Brighton," he announced himself. "Stavion asked me to come along as a little added muscle in case things go downhill. Unlike these assholes, I won't fry in the sun." He laughed when Varik gave him a hard shove against his shoulder, obviously comfortable with the Enforcer.

The other alpha stepped forward and held his hand out as well. "Ridley Thatcher." He shook hands, gave Lynk a nod, and drifted away to settle onto one of the sofas in the sitting room off to the side. The gesture might have been considered rude to some, but Kieran shrugged it off. If there was one thing he'd learned since joining the coven, it was that everyone there had a story.

"Hello," Lynk said quietly, offering a trembling hand.

Xander took the hand gently, clasping it in both massive paws as he smiled reassuringly. "It's nice to meet you, Lynk. My mate, Braxton, speaks very highly of you." He spoke quietly and held Lynk's hand for only a moment before releasing it and giving Kieran a nod, respecting the unwritten boundaries of a mated pair.

"Braxton is your mate?" Lynk's eyes lit up, and the corners of his lips turned up in a half smile. "I met him and Keeton before the meeting last night. They were trying to talk Stavion into building an indoor pool. They're an interesting pair."

Xander chuckled and shook his head. "Separately, they're a handful. Together, they're trouble with a capital *T*. They've already corrupted Malakai, and I have a feeling they'll get Jory and his friends before long. God help us all."

Happy looked good on Lynk, and Kieran loved the way his brown eyes sparkled. From what he'd witnessed, his mate mostly kept to himself, but maybe some new friends were just what he needed to draw him out of his shell. "Maybe Braxton could take Lynk into town when we get back. He needs some new clothes, a coat, and a decent pair of snow boots before winter sets in."

Lynk opened his mouth to argue, but Xander spoke before he could get a word out. "That's more Keeton's area, but I know Braxton wouldn't miss an opportunity to go into town."

Lynk was starting to shake, obviously uncomfortable. Kieran didn't want to sound like an asshole, nor did he want to embarrass his mate by pointing out his edginess, but he needed to do something before Lynk had a panic attack.

Luckily, Xander came to the rescue, doing it with tact and subtly. "I think Aslan said something about Wren outgrowing most of the clothes they have for him. I think he's a little nervous about going into town alone, and Torren can't take time away from The Council right now."

Hearing not only a familiar name, but someone he apparently considered a friend, Lynk relaxed and the trembling subsided. Kieran had an idea a lot of it had to do with Wren as well. He didn't know a single person who could resist the raven-haired pixie. The little boy could charm the birds right from the trees with only a smile.

"Torren would want me to look after his mate," Lynk said after a quiet moment. "If Braxton could drive, I'd be happy to help Aslan and Wren. If that's okay," he added, looking up at Kieran through his eyelashes.

"I know Aslan would appreciate the help." Kieran wound his arm around Lynk's waist and dipped his head at Xander in gratitude for his intervention. "Is Torren here?"

"In the kitchen watching Jory and Wren devour waffles." Varik jerked a thumb over his shoulder. "I never thought I'd meet anyone who loves waffles as much as Jory, but I think Wren has him beat."

Kieran laughed and gave Lynk a little push between his shoulder blades. "You haven't eaten anything since last night. Go get some waffles before they're gone. I'll be there in a minute."

Lynk looked startled but bobbed his head and hurried off to find his brother, leaving Kieran alone with the other men. "I thought you were an elder now," he said to Xander. "How did you get roped into going on this little adventure?"

"Nope." Xander shook his head. "I turned them down. I have no desire to be in charge of anything. I was sworn in as an Enforcer about an hour ago."

"And you, Alpha Thatcher?" Kieran asked Ridley, who was still perched on the sofa, staring off into space. "I know Xander is more alpha by proxy, but you have an entire pack to govern." Maybe it wasn't his place to ask, but that wasn't going to stop him. "Surely your whole pack didn't consent to move to Haven, so why are you here?"

"As of an hour ago, it's Enforcer Thatcher." He shifted around to look at Kieran. "It's only me, my former beta, and two other Enforcers," Ridley answered calmly, though even Kieran could admit that his questioning had been a bit hostile. "The Trinity Pack already has a new alpha, a man I'd trust with my life. They'll be safe and well governed. My reasons for being here are my own, however. As for the other members of my former pack and why they're here, you'll have to ask them."

"Fair enough." Kieran was still curious but understood he wouldn't get more from the shifter just then, so he returned his attention to Xander. "I plan to accompany my mate to Snake River."

"And you'd prefer that I didn't." Xander didn't appear angry. He actually sounded like he'd been expecting the announcement. "I get it, and I hope that you'll eventually come to trust me. I have a mate who I would do anything for, though, so I know where you're coming from. I'll talk to Stavion." Then he strode away, apparently in search of the coven leader.

"He's a good guy," Varik chastised Kieran. "You don't have to be such an insufferable prick."

Kieran respected the friendship Varik had with Xander, but the vampire didn't have a mate of his own, couldn't understand the lengths Kieran would go to in order to protect Lynk. "I'll keep that in mind."

The kicker was that he actually liked Xander. It was just his status as a Moonlighter that was a little harder to reconcile. Since it was looking like the man was going to be a permanent fixture around Haven, Kieran supposed he'd have plenty of time to get to know him and more about his curse, though.

"Kieran, can I have a word?" Torren marched toward him from the direction of the kitchen with a scowl on his face.

He might have been concerned if it wasn't for the fact that Torren always looked half pissed off about one thing or another. "Sure." He moved away from the others and followed the elder halfway down one of the long corridors before the witch came to a stop and faced him. "What's up?"

"Have you had a chance to talk to Blaise?"

"No, there really hasn't been time. Why? Do you know something?" Discovering that Torren hadn't fathered Raina's adopted pups had been a shock. Realizing that there could be someone out there who could claim the twins and take them away from his sister didn't sit well with him, either. They needed to find out one way or another, however, so they could be prepared if that day came.

Torren shook his head slowly. "I've been a little preoccupied myself. Galen says the pups are hybrids, but he can only pick up shifter. That leads me to believe that their father is most likely human. It could be harder to find him if that's the case."

While part of him was pleased by the news because that meant it would be harder for the man to find the twins as well, another part of him felt ashamed at his happiness. It was likely that this guy— whoever he was—didn't even know his children existed. Or worse, he knew and was now somewhere mourning because he thought them dead. However he looked at it, there was a moral obligation on his shoulders that wouldn't let him leave it alone.

"I don't want Raina and Teegan to lose the cubs, but I think we need to find the father. Not only is it the right thing to do, but I can't take the anxiety of constantly waiting for this guy to just pop up. Whatever happens, I want to face it and get it over with."

In a surprise move, Torren clapped him on the shoulder and squeezed in comfort. "You're wrong, you know. You would have made a great leader."

"No. I can take charge when I need to, but I'm not cut out to rule a whole species." He understood his shortcomings and limitations and was fine with them.

He had no regrets about turning down the offer to take the elder seat for the werewolves. Raina was much better suited to that position and would do great things with her new leadership role.

There was something else they needed to discuss, though. "I'm going with Lynk."

Torren bobbed his head and smiled crookedly. "I had a feeling you would. Just…be careful with him."

Kieran remembered Lynk's strange behavior in the shower. "He won't tell me where he was before he was kidnapped. Hell, he practically jumped out of his skin when I asked. I don't know if I can be what he needs."

"You are the other half of his soul—literally. There is no one in the universe better suited to his needs. Take it slow, and you'll get where you need to go."

Well, that was extremely unhelpful. *Leave it to Torren to be all vague and mysterious.* "Give me something, Torren. I don't need to know his life story, but give me some kind of fucking direction. I'm drowning here." It was obvious that Lynk responded to command rather than requests. Kieran just didn't know if that was a good thing or a byproduct of something far more sinister.

"He hasn't told me the full story, either." Torren crossed his arms over his chest and leaned his back against the wall. "I can tell you this. We all have our crosses to bear, the skeletons in our closets if you will. Lynk is probably the most intelligent person I have ever met, but it comes at a price."

"What price?" And more importantly, what could Kieran do to ease his mate's burden?

"You've been stressed lately about finding the man who fathered your nephews, right?" He waited for Kieran's nod. "Your mind is always busy, constantly churning, and you probably only get peace from those thoughts when you sleep."

That was exactly how he felt, but he was still having trouble seeing the point Torren was trying to make. "I don't understand," he finally relented.

"Imagine living your entire life like that—even in sleep. Lynk's mind is in a constant state of chaos, always working, never giving him any peace. It leaves him on edge, nervous, and opens the door for second-guessing and self-doubt."

"How do I help him?" Kieran would do whatever he had to do, be whatever Lynk needed him to be.

"You have to help him shut down and decompress."

"How?"

"I can't tell you that." Pushing away from the wall, Torren paused for just a moment, looking down at his feet before he lifted his head and met Kieran's gaze. "Follow your instincts and do what feels right. Your soul bond will guide you."

"Yeah, okay." Kieran watched the witch walk away and shook his head.

What the fuck was that supposed to mean?

Chapter Five

"Don't take this the wrong way, but why is Torren sending you instead of Raith?"

Lynk folded his hands in his lap and looked over at Kieran as they rode along in the backseat of Varik's SUV. He wasn't offended and could understand why Kieran would question Torren's decision. Raith should have been the obvious choice since he was bigger, stronger, and less likely to get himself hurt if things went wrong.

"I have a connection with Thane. If he's anywhere inside the coven, I'll be able to feel him."

Kieran's brow wrinkled, and his head tilted to the side. "Because he's your brother? Wouldn't Torren or Raith be able to do the same?"

Smiling at his mate's confusion, Lynk shook his head minutely. "Thane is my twin. We can even speak telepathically if we're close enough."

Kieran didn't look pleased about this bit of information, but he didn't comment on it, and Lynk didn't ask. "So, we're trying to find a guy who looks like you?"

"No." Lynk chuckled under his breath at the absurdity that anyone would mistake him for Thane. "He looks more like Torren or Raith. I guess I'm kind of the runt of the family. Well, Sapphire and Silver are small as well, and they're identical, but they have a different mother."

"Wait." Kieran held his hand up as his frown deepened. "There is another set of twins in your family?"

"Four actually. Two sets from our mother, then two sets from our stepmom."

"Okay, so there are thirteen of you. Spell it out for me. I know Torren is the oldest. Then Raith, then you and Thane, but who comes next?" Kieran shook his head and scratched at the back of his neck. "This is going to sound horrible, but again, why you? If Thane is so much bigger, why didn't Torren want us to find him first?"

"Don't worry, Kieran. You're not going to offend me. I'm not sure how it works, but I guess since Thane got the size and strength, I got the magic. I'm quite a bit more powerful than him in that aspect."

Kieran took his hand and squeezed it as he leaned over and kissed Lynk's forehead. "I never doubted your abilities. I'm just trying to understand." He settled back in his seat, but didn't release Lynk's hand. "Okay, so tell me about your brothers. You said there were four sets of twins?"

While he seriously doubted Kieran was that eager to hear about his family tree, Lynk warmed to the idea that his mate was taking an interest in his life. "Okay, so after me and Thane is Mikko."

"Torren said that only Thane could bring Mikko out of Purgatory. I don't understand."

"We're all witches and all powerful, but some of us have extra abilities. Thane can commune with the dead. When a Braddock dies, when one body ceases to breathe and its heart stops beating, another body is born. It's like reincarnation, but we remember our previous lifetimes." Lynk paused, unsure how much he should divulge about how that had come about in the first place.

"And this has to do with you being the keys to the Book of the Banished, right?"

Lynk nodded slowly. "The original circle of thirteen witches tried to destroy the book but was cursed in the process. The book bound itself to the faerie, Camdin. The witches' souls were ripped in two, and half of it sent out into the universe. Those thirteen would always protect the book." Lynk paused, trying to figure out how to finish his abbreviated version of the legend.

"Torren says it's never happened that all thirteen have been born to the same family before," Demos offered from the front passenger seat.

He didn't realize that anyone else knew the story and wondered how many others Torren had told. Part of him also began to panic and prayed that Demos would keep his mouth shut about anything else that he knew. Lynk would eventually have to tell Kieran, but he wasn't ready for that just yet.

Luckily, Demos wasn't one to divulge secrets or offer much in the way of small talk. He settled back into his seat and turned his head to stare out the window. Varik continued driving in silence, not even glancing at them. Ridley was either asleep or doing a good imitation of it in the third-row seat.

Kieran cleared his throat, drawing Lynk's attention back to him. "You lost me again. If Mikko is supposed to be reborn, how is he in Purgatory?"

"Well, because he isn't dead. We won't know how he got trapped there until we get him back and he tells us."

"And why couldn't Aslan get him out?"

"Too dangerous." Lynk shook his head. "Aslan doesn't understand his power yet and can't control it. He could end up letting out the wrong spirit and hurting himself in the process."

"Okay." Kieran paused and a big smile lit his face. "I'll leave the witchy stuff to you because I don't understand most of it. I'll just hit stuff really hard."

Lynk laughed the first real full-out laugh he could remember in so long. "Fair enough."

"So, more about your brothers." Kieran wasn't just asking to make conversation. Lynk could see it in his eyes and the way he leaned forward just slightly that he was really interested. Who had ever been interested in what Lynk had to say?

"Well, Mikko's twin is Nix. Our mother died shortly after they were born, and our father remarried a couple of years later. I don't think either woman was his true mate, though." Lynk shrugged. His father had seemed happy, and that was all that mattered to him.

"Torren said that your stepmom was a shifter."

Lynk bobbed his head. "That's right. She was a jaguar shifter as are my half-brothers. Eris is the oldest of that group. Then the twins Edge and Blade. Sabin was born next, followed by the second set of twins Sapphire, but we call him Phire, and Silver, and finally Indo."

"Interesting names," Kieran commented, but he didn't sound like he was being an ass. "I always wished my name was cooler."

"I like your name. It suits you."

Kieran shrugged. "It's kind of wimpy."

"Not at all. It's a strong name fitting of a warrior. Like I said, it suits you."

His mate might have argued further, but the vehicle began to slow, and Varik announced that they were approaching the front gates of the Snake River Coven. Lynk's stomach tried to twist itself into knots, unheeded by the deep breaths he sucked in to try and calm his racing heart. He didn't want to appear nervous or fearful, but his body was betraying him by slowly coming unglued.

An arm wound around his waist and slid him across the seat until he was pressed right up against Kieran's side. Lynk had been so lost in his frantic thoughts that he hadn't even realized the man had unbuckled his seatbelt. Oh, this was going to go so wrong. They weren't even inside yet, and he couldn't even keep it together.

"Nothing is going to happen to you," Kieran whispered in his ear. "I swear that I won't let anyone touch you."

The words spoken in that deep timbre soothed his frayed nerves like a cool aloe to overheated flesh. The soft lips that brushed over the side of his neck just made his dick hard, but he appreciated the gesture all the same. "Thank you, Kieran."

Kieran brushed Lynk's hair back from his shoulders and nuzzled him just under his jaw. "That's what I'm here for, sugar."

Oh, Lynk was in trouble. He was far too weak where his mate was concerned. He loved the way Kieran always nuzzled him, growled for him, the silly endearments he used. The man was quickly becoming someone Lynk couldn't walk away from, and that could be a problem.

The guards must have been expecting them because one look at Varik, and they just waved them through the gates. The main house loomed ahead of them, not small by any measure, but not nearly as large as the one at Haven. Still, Lynk liked the four huge columns that lined up along the front porch.

"Can you feel anything?" Demos asked, turning in his seat to look at Lynk. He was obviously tense, his eyes wide and alert, ready for trouble. It did nothing to reassure Lynk that they weren't going to end up a midnight snack for the residents of the coven.

The sooner he could determine if his brother was close-by, the quicker they could get the hell out of there. Closing his eyes and drawing on the strength that Kieran offered, Lynk stretched his mind, flexed his magic, and sent out feelers for Thane.

It took approximately half a heartbeat before Lynk's eyes snapped open and he gasped. "He's here."

* * * *

"Shit!" Ridley cursed from the backseat. "This is going to blow goat balls."

Kieran had to agree. While he was glad they'd located Thane Braddock, getting the witch out of the coven was going to be another matter entirely. "What do we do now? It's not like we can just walk in and accuse them of being slime."

"We should go back and let The Council deal with this," Ridley answered. "We know he's here. That should be enough for them to send a whole army of Enforcers in here."

"We are Enforcers, numb nuts." Varik growled and slammed his fist against the steering wheel as he came to a stop in the circle drive just across from the double front doors. "I agree that we can't just go in there and demand that they hand him over, but if we leave now it looks suspicious."

"Do we have a cover story?" Kieran asked. "I mean, is there a reason for us being here?"

"We used to be part of this coven." Demos looked out the window to the enormous house. "We're just coming to see some old friends and see if our old leader has any new information for us about enslaved paranormals."

"Well, then let's get this over with so we can leave." Ridley slapped the back of Kieran's seat. "This place makes me twitchy."

"Everyone just keep your cool and act normal." Varik glanced at them over his shoulder. "The leader is a vampire by the name of October Tuesday."

Kieran snorted while he tried to contain his laughter, but in the end it was just too much. He'd thought the Braddocks had some interesting names, but this guy took the cake. Hell, he knew strippers with less ridiculous names. What the hell had his mother been smoking when she birthed him?

The look Demos leveled on him quieted his mirth instantly. "Don't let his name fool you. He is over a thousand years old and deadly. Do not fuck with him."

"Don't piss off the guy who is named after the month and day he was born on," Kieran recited. "Got it."

"Lord, save me from fools," Varik mumbled. "That is the kind of attitude that will find your head separated from your shoulders. Just keep your mouth closed unless you're asked a question. Now, c'mon."

They all exited the SUV and climbed the front steps as a unit. Before anyone could knock or announce their presence, one of the two doors opened and a tall, too-skinny vampire waved them inside while she smoothed the wrinkles from her dress. "Leader Tuesday is expecting you." She kept her head down, her eyes looking somewhere around their knees as she welcomed them.

No sooner had she spoken the words when Kieran heard several sets of footsteps coming in their direction. Not sure of the coven's stance on same-sex couples and not wanting to embarrass Lynk, Kieran stood close, but kept his hands to himself.

"Demos, Varik, it's so good to see you again!"

If that was Leader Tuesday, he looked damn good for his age. Six-foot give or take with broad shoulders, short blond hair, and a smile straight out of the movies, he was everything most men wanted to be. He just looked kind of fake to Kieran.

Three other vampires flanked him, two bigger and dressed from head to toe in black—obviously the man's personal guards. The man to his left was fairly average in size and appearance. Perhaps the leader's assistant?

"Leader Tuesday," Varik and Demos said in unison as they bowed their heads in respect. Then Varik made the introductions, giving Kieran a warning glare when he said his name.

"Yes, yes, you're all welcome here." Tuesday waved a hand, indicating the men surrounding him. "You remember Axton, Gideon, and Zasha, of course."

None of the men looked happy to be there, but they acknowledged their names with curt nods. All except for the little guy, Zasha, who looked like he'd been clubbed over the head. He was staring in Kieran's direction, but his eyes were glazed as though he wasn't seeing anything or anyone in the room.

Kieran opened his mouth to comment on the odd behavior, but before he could say anything, Zasha flew across the room, faster than Kieran had ever seen anyone move. He had Lynk around the waist and pressed up against his chest in the blink of an eye, jerking his head to the side to expose his neck.

"Mine!" Zasha snarled, right before he sank his fangs into the neck of Kieran's mate.

Chapter Six

Lynk screamed.

He didn't pause to think if it made him look weak or appear less manly. When that vampire douchebag embedded his wicked sharp canines into his neck, it hurt like the seven shades of hell. It also scared the fuck out of him because he was almost certain that Kieran was going to kill the guy.

Protocol forbade a witch from using his or her powers inside another's home unless under duress. Well, having a bloodsucker making a Slurpee out of his neck felt like duress to him. With a few words uttered through gritted teeth, Lynk had the vampire on the floor howling in pain.

The instant he was free, Lynk lifted the spell and hurried to Kieran. It was too late, though. In the four seconds it had taken for Zasha to bite him and Lynk to forcibly remove the guy from his artery, Kieran had apparently lost his damn mind. Lynk was pretty sure it was also bad manners to shift into a seven-foot werewolf in the middle of someone's foyer, but that wasn't stopping his mate.

Russet-colored fur, a long tail, pointed ears, and gleaming daggers that doubled as teeth—Kieran was damn scary. He didn't stalk his prey. He charged the vampire down like a herd of stampeding elephants. Growling and snarling, the pair rolled across the floor, snapping at each other while fists and feet flew in every direction, some connecting on target, other blows missing entirely.

Demos, Varik, Ridley, and both of Tuesday's guards attempted to pry them apart, but ended up being thrown several feet away. When one of the guards pulled a dagger from his belt, Lynk had seen enough. Throwing his hands up in front of him, he froze everyone in place and glared at the Enforcer with the dagger.

"Are you for real? You were going to stab him? I can break your spine with a snap of my fingers." He held his thumb and forefinger together, daring the man to give him a reason to do it. When he felt he had everyone's full attention, he focused his power and released only Kieran from his invisible bonds. "Please shift back."

Gods, he was going to vomit. He hated confrontation of any sort, but seeing Kieran in danger had snapped something inside of him. Now that the situation was under control, he just wanted to go back to being invisible.

Though he looked resistant, Kieran huffed, knelt down on the tiles, and shifted back to his human skin. "I just want to kill him," he whined. "It's just one little vampire. No one will even miss him."

Lynk didn't find the man funny in the least as he rushed forward and threw himself into Kieran's arms. "Are you okay?"

"I should be asking you that." He fingered the bleeding punctures on Lynk's neck and growled. "I need...I can't...I have to..." Rage apparently killed werewolf brain cells and made it impossible for them to form coherent sentences. Luckily, Lynk understood what Kieran was trying to tell him.

Pulling his hair to the side, he tilted his head, offering his neck to his mate. Kieran growled again, his arms tightening around Lynk until he could barely breathe. Though he didn't fully shift, his canines burst through his gums, and his gorgeous blue eyes became an eerie yellow just before he struck.

Kieran's fangs penetrated the skin just over Zasha's mark, erasing any traces of the vampire's claim to Lynk. Where Zasha had caused him only pain, Kieran's bite sent heat spreading through his body until his cock ached with need.

Then his long, slippery tongue lapped over the wound, sealing it so it would heal. He didn't stop there, though. He nuzzled Lynk in a proprietary way, rubbing over every inch of him he could reach. It took Lynk only a second to realize that Kieran was covering him in his scent.

With his very possessive werewolf distracted and unlikely to dismember anyone, Lynk released the rest of the men from his spell, though he kept a firm hold on his mate just in case. Kieran's head snapped up, and he growled viciously when Zasha climbed to his feet and dusted himself off. "Mine!"

Zasha snarled back, prowling a few steps closer before both coven Enforcers grabbed him and held him immobile. "Get your hands off of him!" Zasha demanded, jerking against their hold. "Stop touching my mate!"

"What the hell is going on here?" Leader Tuesday stepped between them and crossed his arms over his chest. "Someone had better start talking." His voice was low, cold, and dripping with threat.

"That man is my mate," Zasha growled.

"Mine!" Kieran roared, clutching Lynk closer to his naked body as his fangs elongated again and sank into the opposite side of Lynk's neck.

There was no stopping his orgasm this time. It slammed into him, steeling his breath as semen shot through his slit to stain the front of his jeans. While he appreciated that Kieran couldn't control his primal instincts, there were just so many times a man could be bitten before the loss of blood became a severe problem.

So, when he could finally make his limbs work again, he slapped at the back of Kieran's head. "Stop that," he mumbled. "They get the point."

Kieran extracted his canines and licked the wound closed but refused to release Lynk. Not that he was complaining since he'd probably end up in a puddle on the floor if Kieran let go of him.

"This is my mate, Kieran Delaney," Lynk said just loud enough for everyone to hear him. "That man"—he pointed at Zasha—"is *not* my mate. I'm pretty sure I'd know if he was." It was so hard to speak in a dignified manner when Zasha was eye-fucking him, Kieran was butt naked, and there was cum cooling on his own dick.

Demos and Varik looked like they wished a hole would open up in the floor and swallow them down. Ridley's face was bright red—probably because he had a hand clamped over his mouth and nose, cutting off his oxygen flow while he tried to control his laughter at the situation.

Leader Tuesday did not look as though he found the situation amusing at all.

"It is common for vampires and werewolves alike to have more than one mate. If Zasha says that you are his, I believe him."

"While that is true of werewolves and vampires," Lynk responded in a subdued tone, "it is not the case for witches, especially a Braddock. I have only one mate, and he's currently licking me like I'm the Thursday Night Special." He swatted at Kieran again where the man was trailing his tongue up the side of his throat. "Focus."

Kieran just made that rumbling sound in his chest somewhere between a growl and purr that made Lynk's cock hard and his pulse race. With his mind tumbling out of control and his body hyperaware of his mate's closeness, Lynk couldn't keep his shields in place any longer. Every scrap of emotion Kieran felt flowed into him, invading his heart, body, and soul.

The wolf in Kieran had taken over, stepping up to defend his position as Lynk's mate. Fury and a fierce possessiveness were the dominant forces, but under that lurked a gentleness, a determination to keep Lynk safe at all costs for he was the only thing that mattered.

He was the quintessential alpha, the man other men wished they could be, and in that moment Lynk realized why they were so perfectly matched for one another.

He needed Kieran's strength, his take-charge and leave-no-prisoners attitude. The structure, the discipline, the control—the caring, understanding, and protection—he craved it, yearned for it, was starved for a little taste of the peace it would bring him. He was a mess, out of control, on a downward spiral into the black abyss, and only Kieran could save him.

Only Kieran could tame him.

Only Kieran Delaney could master him.

"Maybe we should come back another time," Varik said, interrupting Lynk's epiphany.

"No. I believe this is a matter that needs to be settled now." Leader Tuesday wasn't an overly large man, but that didn't make him any less terrifying. A ripple went through the group, a deep shudder like that caused by the frigid winds on a winter's day.

"There is no matter to settle." Ridley pulled himself up to his full, intimidating height and clenched his fists at his sides. "You can't force someone to mate against their will. We're leaving now."

So much venom poured from Ridley, Lynk was surprised the coven leader didn't wither under the poison in his gaze alone. Why the former alpha was standing up for him, he didn't know, but he wasn't about to turn away willing allies. Hell, he wouldn't even turn away *unwilling* allies at this point.

If there was one thing he'd learned from Torren, it was that magic had its time and place. It would be so easy to freeze Tuesday and his guards in place and make a run for it. He couldn't hold them that way forever, though, and sooner or later—and he was betting sooner—they'd all have to face the consequences of his rash actions.

So, he did nothing while he stood in Kieran's embrace and waited for the vampire to make the next move. None of it made any sense to him. Why did Tuesday give a damn about who mated who? Unless, of course, it had something to do with Lynk's last name and the man's desire to have some claim to a Braddock. But he already had Thane. What did he want with Lynk?

Perhaps Tuesday saw him as weak, more easily manipulated by threat and punishment. Because of Lynk's smaller size, it was conceivable that it would prove less daunting to bend him to his will than it would be Thane. And the only reason the coven would want either of them was because of the Book of the Banished.

"Easy," Kieran whispered in his ear. His palm smoothed up and down Lynk's sternum, stroking him like a kitten. "Breathe, baby. I've got you."

Lynk let out the breath he hadn't realized he'd been holding and melted back into Kieran's arms, soaking up his confidence. How had things gone so wrong so quickly? They hadn't even made it past the foyer for pity's sake.

"I'm not forcing anyone to do anything," Tuesday replied to Ridley's accusation after a long pause. "We have a very unusual circumstance here, and I simply wish to get to the bottom of it. Finding one's mate should be a time of celebration. We are drawn to our other halves. It's unlikely that Zasha has made a mistake in thinking Mr. Braddock is his mate."

"Well, it's Lynk's word against Fang Boy's over there." Ridley waved dismissively at Zasha. "There's no way to prove who is telling the truth."

"Ah, but there is."

"How?" Ridley, Lynk, and Kieran all asked in stereo.

"If Lynk is Zasha's true mate, he will be immune to Zasha's compulsion."

Technically, the vampires in the room could only compel him if he allowed it. While it wasn't exactly on his bucket list, Lynk figured he could allow it this one time if it meant proving that he belonged with Kieran.

Even as he had the thought, another chased right on its heels. What if it was a setup? What if the entire scene had been orchestrated so that it would lead up to this moment? Zasha attacked him, bit him, and claimed to be his mate. Now the only way to prove him false was for Lynk to allow the guy to compel him.

What if it was all just a clever ruse designed to force the whereabouts of the Book of the Banished from him? If Lynk allowed it, they would have the information they wanted. If he refused, he looked guilty. If he agreed then blocked Zasha out of his mind, it looked as though he was the vampire's true mate.

It was a clever ploy, but Lynk was on to them now. Why else would Leader Tuesday stick his nose into such a trivial personal matter? And why the hell were Varik and Demos just standing there, not saying a damn word in his defense?

"Wait," Varik said, stepping forward with both hands raised. Though he'd wanted this, Lynk still had to resist the urge to put a gag spell on him in fear that he'd say something to make the situation even worse. "What about Kieran? Doesn't he get the chance to prove that Lynk is his mate as well?"

"Yes," Tuesday answered tightly. "It is only fair, I suppose."

Okay, great, something was finally going their way. "How do we prove it?" he whispered up to his mate.

Kieran's entire body was as rigid as stone, and he'd begun to growl like a rabid dog. "No."

"If Kieran fails his test, then Zasha will have a chance to prove himself as Lynk's true mate." Well, at least Demos finally had something helpful to say.

"No!" Kieran spat. "We are leaving. If you come anywhere near him, I will shred each and every one of you with my bare hands and laugh while I do it."

"Zasha has staked a claim to Lynk." Tuesday looked much too pleased for Lynk's liking. "Until it is proven that you are not coercing Mr. Braddock into denying his bond with Zasha, he will remain here." He looked around their loosely formed circle. "You *all* will remain here."

"You can't keep us here!" Ridley shouted.

Tuesday chuckled darkly and shook his head. "My boy, I can do anything I want. Axton, Gideon, please show our guests to their rooms."

"Fuck this." Kieran lifted Lynk into his arms and swung around toward the front doors, only to find them barricaded by a dozen Enforcers.

Knowing there would be serious consequences, but not seeing any other way out of their predicament, Lynk concentrated all of his power, sending a blast of magic through the room to bind the Snake River vampires in place.

"Hurry." Varik ushered them through the doors and out to his SUV. "Shit, shit, shit!"

"We are so completely screwed," Demos added as he slid into the passenger seat.

"Fuck that tool," Ridley called from the very back of the vehicle. Not exactly eloquent, nor was it in any way helpful, so Lynk ignored him.

"What are we going to do now?"

"We're going straight to Casper, and you're going to tell Torren everything that happened," Varik said as he stomped on the accelerator.

"Why me?" Lynk demanded.

Demos glanced over his shoulder and shrugged. "Because he won't kill *you*."

Chapter Seven

"You did what?" Torren bellowed.

Kieran—dressed in an extra pair of clothes from his backpack—pushed Lynk behind him and faced the elder with a look of contempt. "What the hell did you want him to do?" It didn't matter if Torren was Lynk's brother. No one talked to his mate like that.

"Can't we bring charges against him for trying to force Lynk into a mating?" Ridley asked.

Torren pushed his hair back from his forehead and groaned. "I don't know. We'll have to talk to Elder Cortez. I don't know all the rules of vampire society. Sloan would be able to tell us more."

"Thane is there," Lynk said quietly, trying to push around Kieran and huffing when Kieran refused to let him. "The connection is weak, but it's there. I'd guess he's being sedated."

"Am I the only one that found Zasha's display of possession a little too convincing?" Demos shrugged when Kieran growled at him. "It didn't look like a setup. It felt real."

"Well, his teeth in my neck certainly felt real."

Kieran wrapped his arm around Lynk's shoulders and pulled him closer to his side. Just thinking about the bloodsucker biting his mate was enough to make him shake in rage. There was also a small part of him that felt guilty. He'd promised to keep Lynk safe, swore that no one would touch him. Within five minutes of stepping foot inside that house, he'd broken his promise.

It had all happened so fast, though. One minute they were playing nice and making introductions, and the next, Zasha had Lynk pressed up against him and was making a snack out of his jugular. Everything after that was a bit of a blur, but Kieran still felt the urge to snap the fucker in half and twist him into a pretzel.

"It's possible that he truly thought Lynk was his mate," Torren said after a long minute of silence. He slid into one of the kitchen chairs and motioned for everyone else to do the same. Apparently this was going to be a long discussion.

"But, he's not," Lynk said as Kieran settled the man into his lap. He was more than a little pleased when his mate didn't argue with him. "Why would he think that?"

Torren pinched the bridge of his nose and closed his eyes, though he looked like he wanted to slam his forehead against the kitchen table. "He could be Thane's mate. As your twin, your energies are very similar. The connection between the two of you was still open when this vampire came close to you. It's possible that he's feeling Thane through you."

"Oh, fuck me running," Raith groaned. "So, what do we do now? Can't we just go in there and take Thane?"

"We don't know where he's being held," Torren argued.

"Lynk can find him."

"They'll never let us take him without a fight."

"You're a goddamn elder!" Raith exploded. "Why are you backing down from this?"

"Snake River is one of the biggest covens in the country," Torren replied calmly. "We don't have enough Enforcers to fight them, and we have no evidence to arrest anyone."

"We know Thane is there."

"Prove it," Torren returned with an arched eyebrow.

"Why do we have to prove anything?" Kieran demanded. They'd rescued plenty of captives on little more than a hunch or a tipoff. Why was this any different? He was willing to bet everything he owned that Thane Braddock wasn't the only person being held against his will in Snake River.

Torren looked exhausted right down to his bones as he stared at Kieran. It was understandable considering how quickly things were snowballing downhill for the paranormal world. The witches who had tried to attack them during their Halloween gathering were only the beginning. More would come, and the next time, they'd come prepared.

They were still trying to find the remaining Braddock brothers. More captives were being reported all around the country. There were still missing children and more turning up drained of their powers courtesy of different power-hungry witch covens. It was a lot of responsibility to shoulder.

"I'm not sure it would matter if we had proof," Torren said quietly. "Snake River has more Enforcers than the whole of The Council. That's not even counting the number of coven guards who aren't registered Enforcers. That place is locked down tighter than Alcatraz."

Varik and Demos sat with their heads down and their hands clenched on the table in almost identical poses. "We didn't know," Varik mumbled. "I swear we didn't know."

"No one is blaming you," Torren assured them.

Kieran didn't blame them, either, but Varik's comment did spark another thought. "If you guys didn't know, then it's possible that no one else does. What if it's only a small faction like Tuesday's inner circle?"

"That's a good point." Torren's brow creased even as he rubbed at it with his fingertips as though trying to iron out the wrinkles. "I'll get in touch with the other elders and call a special meeting for later tonight."

"Daddy," a quiet, sleepy voice called from the doorway. Wren stood there, clutching the ugliest stuffed pig Kieran had ever seen. "I had a bad dream."

"Everyone is welcome to stay," Torren said as he moved around the table and lifted his son into his arms. "You want to tell me about your dream, buddy?"

Wren shook his head, wrapped his arms around Torren's neck, and buried his little face in Torren's throat. "Will you tell me a story?"

Aslan wandered into the kitchen, yawning hugely as he waved his hello to everyone. "You want me to take him so you can finish up here?" he asked his mate.

Torren bent and kissed him on the forehead. "We're done." His fingers looped around the back of Aslan's neck and squeezed lightly. "C'mon, sleepyheads. Let's get you two back in bed."

The trio disappeared, but Kieran continued to stare at the spot where they'd been, unable to swallow around the lump in his throat. He wanted that. While he had his siblings, and now his sister's twins, he wanted a family of his own.

Taking Lynk's hand, he brought it to his lips and whispered a kiss over the knuckles. They'd get there one day. It had been barely three days since they'd met, and there were still a multitude of issues to work out in their relationship before they got to that point.

"We're going to head back to Haven," Demos announced. "Someone needs to fill Stavion in on what happened."

"And we need to prepare for any backlash against Haven," Ridley added, rising to his feet with the vampires. "Do you need anything from your place, Kieran?"

"That would be great. I'll call Parker and have him get it together if you don't mind grabbing it before the meeting tomorrow."

"No problem. We'll see you guys later." Then they were gone as well, leaving Kieran alone with his mate for the first time since the sun had set.

"Do you want me to stay?" He probably should have thought to ask his mate that before everyone left. Still, there were plenty of spare rooms and even a few couches if it came down to it.

"Of course I want you to stay." Lynk looked at him in shock. "Why would you think differently?"

Because I'm insecure and you confuse the hell out of me. "I just wanted to be certain that we were on the same page. So, which room is yours?"

Lynk rose to his feet, took Kieran's hand, and tugged him gently. "I'll show you."

* * * *

Snuggled in bed, his head resting on his mate's chest, Lynk voiced the question that had been weighing on his mind since the fiasco at Snake River. "How would you prove that we're mates? Why did you get so angry about it?"

Kieran sighed and hugged him closer. "They'd have to separate us on the full moon. I don't trust those idiots. There was no way I was letting them take you away from me."

"What would happen on the full moon?" Lynk curled closer and smiled, warmed that Kieran wanted to keep him close.

"I'd shift, find you, and claim you. It can be very intense, and a werewolf will do whatever it takes to get to his mate on a full moon. It can be physically painful for me if I don't find and claim you."

"So, I need to stick close on the full moon."

"That would be appreciated." Kieran rolled to his side and tilted Lynk's head up with gentle pressure under his chin. "It can be scary. I'll claim you in my shifted form, and I'll probably be pretty growly. It's still me, though, and I would never do anything to hurt you, okay?"

"When you claim me…that includes sex, right?" Kieran dipped his head once, never taking his eyes from Lynk's. Lynk had seen his mate in shifted form, and he had serious doubts that the monster cock between his powerful thighs would fit, but he was more than up to the

were still things to be said, things that might have Kieran rethinking wanting to bind himself to Lynk forever.

Pushing at his lover's chest, Lynk jerked his mouth away and panted for a moment before he could get enough air into his lungs to speak. "Wait. I...There's more that I need to tell you. About my life before I came here."

"It doesn't matter." Kieran chased his lips again, but Lynk turned his head, fighting against his desire to just shut up and let his mate ravish him.

"It does matter. You need to know everything before I claim you." His heart pounded wildly, and his body trembled with nerves. The things he secretly craved in the dark of night had driven a wedge between them once before. If it was destined to happen again, he wanted to know up front before his heart was too invested.

"Lynk, I've already claimed you. Nothing you can say is going to make me walk away from you. Don't push this. You're not ready, but you'll tell me when you are."

"I can't take it back once I claim you. I have to tell you now before that happens," Lynk argued, losing his courage with every passing moment.

"I can't take it back, either. You're stuck with me."

Realizing the words were true, a little piece of Lynk's heart died. How long before the rest of it shattered as well?

Chapter Eight

He didn't know what he'd said wrong, but he'd obviously screwed up somehow. Lynk was so stiff, his muscles tense, and his joints locked. He'd also gone very quiet and wouldn't look Kieran in the eye any longer.

"Lynk, look at me," he coaxed, stroking the side of his lover's face. "Tell me what's wrong."

"Maybe it can wait."

Two minutes ago, Kieran would have agreed. Now, he wanted to know what the hell was going on in Lynk's pretty little head. Whatever it was, it had him all tied up in knots, and that just wouldn't do. "You can tell me anything."

He didn't want to push and make his lover uncomfortable, but there seemed to be a big stone wall constructed between them. Until he could tear it down, he had no hope of having the type of relationship with Lynk that he wanted.

"Can I promise to tell you later?" Lynk reached out tentatively and skimmed his fingertips down the valley between Kieran's chest muscles. It was the first contact he'd initiated between them, and Kieran couldn't suppress the shiver that rushed up his spine.

"Lynk." He tried to speak firmly, but the single word rushed out on a shuddering breath as his cock swelled and his pulse galloped.

Since first catching Lynk's intoxicating scent on the front steps of the house, he'd been beating back his basic instincts to fully claim his mate—inside and out. While Lynk bore his mating mark on his neck, it wasn't enough. Kieran's beast was howling to have their mate beneath them, naked, moaning, and writhing, delirious with pleasure from their touch.

"When the time is right," Lynk whispered, craning his neck up to capture Kieran's lips. "I promise I'll tell you soon, Kieran. Please." His slippery tongue swirled around the jumping vein in Kieran's neck. "I need you."

While part of him recognized that he was being manipulated, Kieran really didn't give a damn. According to Lynk, they had eternity to share the secrets of their pasts. Whatever was lurking in the dark places of Lynk's mind, Kieran would eventually ferret it out. The trick was to take it one day at a time, prove himself worthy of his lover's trust. Everything else would fall into place as they went.

"Please, sir," Lynk whispered against Kieran's jaw.

The quiet plea snapped him, and a primal growl rumbled in his chest as he pinned Lynk back to the mattress and attacked his mouth with a savage intensity. One hand fisted in his mate's hair to hold him in place while the other made quick work of removing Lynk's boxers, shredding them until the scraps fell away to leave only smooth, tanned skin.

"I could have done that," Lynk panted before diving back into the kiss. In the next heartbeat, Kieran's boxers vanished, and he groaned into his lover's mouth when their heated flesh met.

As much as he was enjoying himself, they needed to move things forward or he was going to blow before they even got to the good stuff. He'd been wound so tight, trying to keep his desire in check, and now that he'd been given the okay to unleash it, he was quickly spiraling out of control.

Thankfully, Lynk didn't seem to mind, if the moans and whimpers pouring from him were any indication. His lean muscles flexed and stretched as he squirmed on the bed, rocking his pelvis so that their hard cocks grinded together.

A thin sheen of perspiration glistened over his supple skin, making him almost glow in the soft light from the bedside lamp. In that moment, with his face flushed and his eyes closed, his mind obviously lost in pleasure rather than whirling with doubts and worries, he was flawless. Kieran had never seen a more perfect creation in all of his life.

While he lost himself in his contemplation of his lover, Lynk rolled to his side and fished around in the drawer of the nightstand, coming back with a barely used bottle of lube that he offered up to Kieran like a virgin sacrifice. "I can stretch myself if you want."

What a ridiculous question. "Why would I miss an opportunity to touch you, sugar?" He grabbed the little bottle and clutched it in his fist before crushing their lips together again and delving inside for another taste of the moist depths of Lynk's mouth.

"Please, sir," Lynk practically sobbed. "Please, hurry."

Kieran didn't understand his mate's desire to call him sir, but he couldn't deny that it did explosive things to his libido. That was something they'd have to discuss—much, much later. "Quiet, baby. Let me take care of you."

Lynk quieted instantly, and his body relaxed as the most blissful expression settled over his face. Happy to be able to put that smile on his man's face, Kieran shimmied down Lynk's body, trailing open-mouth kisses over his damp skin. Those little, brown nipples called out to him, practically begging to be sucked, nipped, and lavished with attention.

When he had one nipple standing at attention, swollen and red from his attention, he moved on to the next while he used his hands to knead the yielding flesh around Lynk's hips. His mate made the most enticing noises when he forgot to be all proper and high-strung. Though his cock was hard as stone and leaking freely from the slit, Kieran was more than happy to ignore his own needs and shower attention on his lover.

Moving farther down Lynk's body, Kieran swirled his tongue around the man's belly button and lapped at each brick of hard abdominal muscle. His sculpted body was a treasure, and at the moment, it was Kieran's playground. He'd never seen so many beautiful muscles on such a small man before.

While he wasn't normally attracted to large men like himself, he had always had a fascination with muscles. It had been quite the dilemma until Lynk had popped into his life. It was as though he'd been made just for Kieran, molded to be his every fantasy and desire come to life.

As he worshiped the man's body with his tongue, he flipped open the cap on the lube and slathered his fingers with the gel. Urging his mate's legs wider with his shoulders, he skimmed the crease of Lynk's ass before pushing between the rounded globes and zeroing in on his quivering pucker.

Groaning against Lynk's stomach, he ringed the twitching muscles, coaxing them to relax until he could insert one finger into the tight, heated channel. He pumped lazily, stretching Lynk's hole while he flicked his tongue over the head of his dripping cock. His man went wild, jerking and bucking, impaling himself on Kieran's digit. His cries of pleasure rose in volume, bouncing off the ceiling and walls and right back to Kieran's ears like a sweet symphony.

"Please," Lynk begged. "I can take it. Please, take me, sir."

While he was sure that Lynk would be a perfect fit for him, wrapping around his steel-hard cock like a glove, he wouldn't rush, wouldn't do anything to even inadvertently hurt his lover. "Quiet," he ordered again as he inserted a second finger and enveloped the engorged crown of Lynk's cock in his mouth.

"Oh, cheese and crackers!" Lynk yelled.

Kieran chuckled around the pulsing flesh in his mouth. He'd never heard that particular curse during the throes of passion, but as long as his lover was enjoying himself, Lynk could scream whatever he wanted.

Wondering what other strange sayings Lynk had in his repertoire, he pushed in with a third finger. At the same time, he took his mate's cock to the back of his throat and swallowed around the tip.

"Fish sticks, fudge, motherclucker, son of a monkey!"

Oh, lord, Kieran couldn't remember the last time he'd laughed so much during sex. It was the cutest damn thing he'd ever heard, and it only made him want Lynk that much more. Popping off of his lover's cock, he buried his face in the crease of Lynk's thigh and chuckled softly as he continued to work his fingers in and out of Lynk's snug channel.

When he had all three fingers gliding seamlessly without resistance, he eased out and positioned himself so that he was kneeling between Lynk's trembling legs, gripping the base of his dick to stave off his orgasm. It did nothing to help his composure when Lynk looped his arms under his knees and pulled his legs back to his chest, placing his slicked hole on clear display.

"Ah, fuck, Lynk." Kieran's breath lodged in his chest as he surged forward, encasing himself in Lynk's heated tunnel.

"Yes, yes, fuck Lynk," his mate babbled adorably while his head whipped back and forth on the pillow and his fingers clutched at Kieran's shoulders.

Lynk's inner walls convulsed around his length, squeezing and massaging until Kieran thought his eyes would cross. "Damn, you're tight." He pulled all the way out, teased Lynk's hole with the tip of his cock, and then surged back in to the root. He did it again. And again.

"Oh, oh, oh," Lynk chanted. His cock jerked between them, rising up before slapping against his stomach and coating his skin in clear drops of pre-cum. "I'm gonna come. Please, may I come, sir?"

"No," Kieran growled. "Don't you dare come until I say you can." He didn't understand why Lynk would ask him such a question. He understood even less why he'd denied his lover. Most of the blood in his body had pooled in his cock, leaving little in his brain for such things as coherent thought process.

There were clues there, pieces of the puzzle that would give him a deeper look into what Lynk needed from him. He just couldn't focus long enough to put them together.

Every hard thrust into Lynk's welcoming body sent him a little closer to the edge of the cliff. His balls ached as his sac drew up tight to his body. His cock swelled and throbbed inside Lynk's hole, and nothing mattered but seeing that look of pleasure-pain on his lover's face.

Lynk's abs tightened, the cords in his neck strained, and his dick flexed with the pounding of his heart. It was obvious that he needed release, but Kieran's refusal seemed to spur him on, driving his lust higher. His eyes were wide open, as big around as dinner plates, and staring up at Kieran as though he'd roped the moon and presented it to Lynk with a pretty red bow.

No one had ever looked at him that way before—as though he wasn't just the most important person on earth, but the *only* person in the cosmos. He didn't know what to do with that level of devotion, so he pushed it to the back of his mind to ponder later.

Sweat beaded across his forehead, dampened his hair, and rolled down his chest and back. His heart thundered against his ribs, his skin tingled, and tiny explosions detonated through his body. Harder, faster, he surged into Lynk's ass, pounding him into the mattress with enough force to rattle his own bones.

Lynk cried out, dug his short nails into Kieran's back, and begged for more. Just before his orgasm overtook him, Kieran felt his fangs burst through his gums, and his eyes shifted so that everything existed in monochrome. He tried to shake it off, to subdue his wolf, but it was a hopeless battle.

"Please," Lynk whispered, tilting his head to the side submissively as he urged Kieran's mouth to his neck. "I need it."

With a loud roar, Kieran embedded his canines in the apex of Lynk's shoulder, growling like a wild beast at the first rush of blood over his tongue. His eyes closed against his will, his body tensed, and his cock erupted as the most mind-numbing orgasm barreled into him like a locomotive.

Pumping furiously through what felt like a never-ending climax, Kieran extracted his fangs and licked over the mark. "Come," he grunted, barely able to say the one word before another shock of electricity raced up his spine.

Lynk screamed until the windows shook, and his cock discharged between them, coating his chest and abs in rivers of hot, sticky seed. Words spilled from his lips in a language that Kieran didn't understand, and he figured it was just more incoherent babbling until it suddenly felt like the sun itself had exploded inside his chest.

"Lynk!" He screamed, actually screamed, while his body went into convulsions, his hips jerked, slamming his cock deeper into Lynk's body, and he erupted once again. Just before his world went dark and he was sucked into the void, he heard Lynk whispering to him over the beating of his heart and the panting of his breath.

"Given freely. Two hearts as one. I bind myself to you. Offer all that I am and the pledge of my eternal love."

Deciding that sounded pretty damn good to him, Kieran had just enough consciousness left to collapse to the side of his lover, and then everything floated away.

Chapter Nine

"This stops now. I won't keep doing this!"

"Please, sir. What did I do wrong? Just tell me what I did wrong." Lynk knelt on the floor with his hands resting on his thighs and his head bent. He tried and tried, wracking his brain for some infraction that could be causing his Master to be angry with him.

"You didn't do anything wrong." Kieran sighed and dropped his head, pushing his hand through his waist-length hair. He was completely nude, his soft cock still shiny with spit from Lynk's mouth. The candlelight played over his muscles, highlighting their definition and making Lynk's mouth water for just one more taste.

His eyes, however, were shadowed, hard, and maybe just a little sad. *"I don't understand,"* Lynk whispered. *"If you could just tell me what I did to displease you."*

"Do you love me, Lynk?"

Lynk tilted his head to the side, confused by the question. *"I worship you, sir. You are everything to me."*

Apparently, this was the wrong answer, because Kieran growled and slammed his fist into the wall of their little log cabin. *"I don't want you to worship me. There is more to life than me, Lynk. I shouldn't be your everything. Don't you want anything for yourself?"*

"I want you," Lynk answered honestly. What else was there? He'd dedicated the last three years of his life to pleasing his lover, mate, and Master.

"What else?" Kieran asked almost pleadingly. *"What else do you want?"*

He was growing more confused by the moment. "I don't want anything. You are all I need."

"No!" Kieran roared and his body began to vibrate. "What are you going to do when I'm not around anymore?"

"W–What? Where are you going?" Lynk resisted the urge to jump to his feet and throw himself at his mate. "Why won't you be here?"

Kieran dropped his head so that his chin rested on his chest and fisted his hands on his hips as he sighed heavily. "I'm not going anywhere, but we don't know what could happen. What if I died tomorrow, Lynk? What would you do then?"

"No." Lynk shook his head firmly. "You won't die. I won't let you. We're bonded. Together forever."

"I can't keep hurting you, Lynk. It's killing me. I don't understand what you need, and you won't tell me. I just know that I can't do this anymore."

"But I need it!" Lynk cried. "It's the only way to make everything go away. It's the only time I get any peace!"

Kieran didn't say anything while he pulled on his trousers and laced them. He didn't even bother with a shirt or shoes as he crossed the room and paused in the doorway where he spoke without turning. "I'm sorry, Lynk." Then he walked away, leaving Lynk alone, still kneeling on the floor in the middle of the room.

He wasn't sure how much time passed while he sat there in numb silence. All he knew was that his life was over. If Kieran didn't come back, nothing else mattered. While he stared blankly at the wall, a shiver raced up his spine as he was blasted with a wave of magic not his own.

Panic seized him, and he jumped to his feet, dashing out of the room, unconcerned with his nudity. "Kieran!" He ran as fast as he could through the house to the wide-open front door, but he wasn't fast enough.

Lynk came awake with a scream, panting for breath while tears streamed down his cheeks. It had been years since he'd had that particular dream, but it was still just as painful as though he'd lived it only moments before.

When his mate's hand smoothed down his spine, he flipped over and burrowed into Kieran's arms, clinging to his neck as though the big werewolf would disappear if he didn't keep a strong hold on him. "I'm so sorry," he breathed against the side of his mate's neck. "I wasn't fast enough. I should have never let you leave like that. I'm sorry, Kieran."

Kieran petted his hair, stroking it back from his face. It was only then that Lynk realized his lover was holding him just as tightly while his big frame trembled and his breathing came fast and shallow against Lynk's temple. The fingers on his other hand dug into Lynk's hip, gripping him hard enough to leave bruises.

"I was coming back," he whispered shakily. How fitting that they'd been having the same dream. "I just needed air, needed to think. I was so young back then, and I didn't understand. I get it now, Lynk. I know what I have to do. I won't mess it up this time. Please forgive me."

If anyone should be begging forgiveness, it was Lynk. He was the one who'd pushed his young mate too far. He'd been nearly fifteen years older than Kieran's twenty-two years back in the 1600s. Lost in his own selfishness, he hadn't seen what he'd been doing to Kieran then. He'd pressed too hard, asked too much.

Kieran had always been so much bigger and stronger than him, but it was Lynk's job to protect his *Infinity*. Kieran was a treasure, a gift given to him by the fates, and instead of nurturing and cherishing that gift, he'd neglected it. That wouldn't happen again.

His lover wasn't the only one to have an epiphany about past mistakes. Lynk understood precisely where he'd gone wrong and what he needed to do differently this time around.

"You have nothing to be sorry for, love." He stroked Kieran's hair, his shoulders, and down his back. The roles had reversed, and he now found himself the comforter. Surprisingly, it was a position in which he was completely comfortable. As much as he needed Kieran, he was beginning to realize that Kieran needed him as well.

There was a reason they were meant for each other. From their shared souls and their past lives all the way to the present moment, they were so intricately connected, each designed solely for the other. It was the reason that none of their past relationships had worked, why everything felt hollow and superficial.

"They were witches, weren't they?" Kieran asked. "I only made it to the front lawn when I realized how immature I was acting. They stepped out of the trees just as I turned around to go back inside."

Lynk swallowed hard and dipped his head once. "Yes, they were witches. They wanted the Book of the Banished." That book had caused so much trouble for so long. There had to be a way to destroy it. They just had to find it. "I came for you when I felt the magic in the air, but I wasn't fast enough. I watched the dagger sink into your chest and wanted to die." Lynk dropped his head and squeezed his eyes closed. "They gave me my wish when I wouldn't tell them where the book was."

Kieran didn't reply, seemingly lost in thought, and Lynk went back to gliding his fingertips along his lover's spine. They'd both made mistakes in the past, but that didn't mean that history had to repeat itself. Lynk wouldn't let it.

"It's kind of like I've been playing a game," Kieran mused, his muscles finally relaxing under Lynk's attention. "Do you know what I mean?"

Not a clue. "Tell me."

"Well, it's like I've never really fit anywhere. I've always taken care of my siblings, and I was the beta of my old pack. I've done what I was supposed to do for my entire life, but I've always just kind of felt like a zombie." He cuddled Lynk closer and nuzzled against him. "I don't feel like that anymore."

"I don't feel like that, either." While he didn't fully understand what Kieran's life had been like, he did know about feeling empty and misplaced.

Claiming Kieran was like coming home. It didn't necessarily change the things he craved, but it did give him a sense of completeness that he'd been missing. Somehow, someway, he'd figure out how to curb his desires. Things would work this time. Everything would be perfect.

A feeling of protectiveness washed over him, something he'd never felt for anyone except his brothers. It didn't make a lot of sense. Kieran didn't need protection, especially not from someone so much smaller than him. It was there all the same, though.

"Do you remember when I taught you how to swim?"

Lynk blinked several times before he burst into laughter. "It was the middle of November, and you threw me in the river. I don't think that exactly counts as 'teaching' me to swim."

"Hey," Kieran replied indignantly. "I came in after you, didn't I?"

"I almost drowned, you idiot."

Kieran chuckled and rolled them so that he loomed over Lynk. "You still loved me, though."

His smile softened as he reached up to cup Kieran's cheek. "I never stopped. It's been a long time, and I've lived several lives, but I never forgot you." He carded his fingers through Kieran's short hair. "I did like the longer hair, though."

"Then I'll grow it out." Kieran said it seriously, and Lynk knew he wasn't kidding.

Part of him wanted to tell his lover that it didn't matter what he looked like or how he wore his hair. He'd really loved those long, silky locks, though. So he just smiled and kept his mouth shut.

"Can I ask you something?"

"You can ask me anything." Kieran rubbed his cheek over Lynk's palm for a moment before he dipped his head and brushed their lips together. "What do you want to know?"

"How did you end up in Haven? You said you were the beta for your pack."

"My dad is the alpha, and he's a bastard," Kieran said matter-of-factly. "Pack members were beaten to death for being gay. Cubs were taught to distrust and hate anyone but other werewolves. When my sister and Teegan met and realized they were mates, we had to keep it a secret for a long time."

"That's horrible." Lynk couldn't imagine having to hide how much Kieran meant to him.

"It is. Well, our mother caught them together one day, and she's not any better than our father. We've always stuck together and looked out for each other, so when shit went down, we ran. We hid out for a while until we heard rumors about a place where people were accepted and everyone was taken care of. We sniffed around the place for a few days until I finally made the decision to talk to Stavion. He gave us a home, and for that, I'll always be indebted to him."

"I lived south of where they found me in that slaughterhouse in a place near Lake Erie." His mouth was dry and his throat constricted, trying to keep him from speaking, but Lynk pushed on, anyway. After what Kieran had just shared, it was only fair for him to divulge his past as well. Besides, they couldn't move forward in their relationship until all the cards were on the table.

"I'm going to guess you didn't live alone."

Lynk didn't think he imagined the growl in Kieran's voice, but it wasn't like his jealous lover had been a choirboy before they'd met, either. "No, I didn't live alone. It was my Master's house. He took care of me, paid for everything, bought me whatever I needed."

"Master?" Kieran sneered the word with so much contempt that it left Lynk feeling cold. "Like how you used to call me Master?"

Lynk nodded slowly. He knew Kieran had always hated the term, but to Lynk it had been a form of endearment.

"And what did he call you, sugar?"

"Slave," Lynk responded quietly. "That's what I was. He wasn't kind like you were. He was human. I couldn't risk getting involved with another paranormal. I didn't realize that he had connections in our world, though. One minute we're sipping champagne on the balcony, and the next, I'm face down in the dirt in that slaughterhouse."

"How long were you there?"

"A couple of weeks, I think, but I can't really be sure. They kept me sedated, so everything just kind of blurred together after the first few days."

"I'm going to go run," Kieran said after a long silence. He bent his head again to kiss Lynk's lips. "I'm not running away, though. There's a lot of shit going on inside my head right now, and running helps me think. You stay right here where it's safe and keep the bed warm for me. I'll be back in an hour or so."

Lynk bit his bottom lip and bobbed his head slowly. The last time Kieran had gone out for some air, it had ended in tragedy. He couldn't keep sitting around waiting for bad things to happen, though. It wasn't like he could lock his lover in the room and never let him leave. "Please be careful."

"I promise." Kieran slid off the bed and pulled his jeans on, leaving them unbuttoned so that it showed just a hint of his groin. "I'm coming back, Lynk. Try to get some sleep."

He must have still looked reluctant, because Kieran eased down on the side of the bed and pinched his chin between thumb and forefinger. "Look at me, sugar." He waited for Lynk to meet his eyes before continuing. "Who takes care of you?"

"You do."

"That's right. Do you trust me?"

"Yes, sir."

"Then trust me when I tell you that I'm going to be fine. I'm not some dumb kid like last time. I want you to take a hot shower then snuggle under the blankets and sleep until I get back." His grin was cocky as he stood from the bed and arched an eyebrow. *"And if you really need me, just yell."*

"How did you do that?" Lynk scrambled to a sitting position, his mouth hanging open like a guppy. "I heard you in my head."

"I can hear you, too, ya know. Give it a try."

"Why didn't you ever tell me before? Why didn't I know about this the last time we were together?"

Kieran chuckled under his breath and shook his head. "I was human last time we were together, sugar. Being a werewolf has its perks, though. Now do what I said, and I'll be back soon."

"Same goes for you," Lynk ordered. "If you need me, I'll be there. I'll be fast enough this time." Hopefully he wouldn't be put to the test so soon after finding his mate again, but if the need arose, he'd be ready this time. They were facing a lot of bad shit in their future, but Lynk wasn't going to lose Kieran for a second time.

Kieran just winked and disappeared out into the hallway. He couldn't have made it far when Lynk heard him inside his head, though. *"Hey, sugar?"*

"Yes, Kieran?" Lynk grinned to himself at his mate's playfulness. For as fierce as he was, it was unexpected, but not unwelcome.

"I never stopped loving you, either. I just didn't realize it until now."

Chapter Ten

"How do propose that we gain allies within the Snake River Coven?" Elder Cortez addressed the members of the meeting from his chair on the dais.

Kieran honestly had no interest in the meeting or in gaining allies. The only reason he was there was to support Lynk. As an Enforcer, it would be his job to help rescue anyone being held prisoner in Snake River. As Lynk's mate, it was his job to endure these boring meetings and pretend like he was interested when in actuality, someone could just brief him after everything was said and done.

"This has to do with you as well, you know. I'm sure Elder Tuesday is going to try to use Zasha's supposed claim to me as leverage. I don't know what he hopes to accomplish with that bit, though."

It took every ounce of willpower he had not to growl like an animal, snatch Lynk up and scream, "Mine!" Kieran managed, though, settling for a grunt of annoyance instead. Let someone try to take his mate away from him. He dared them.

"You're very sexy when you get all jealous," Lynk observed, pushing his thoughts into Kieran's mind.

"I'm not jealous. I'm...territorial."

"Yes, sir," Lynk responded, but Kieran could see the corners of his lips twitch as though he was fighting a smile.

After arriving home after his run, he'd found Lynk freshly showered and sleeping peacefully, all snuggled down in the blankets. It had been such a heartwarming sight that he'd stood beside the bed for a long time, just watching his lover sleep. Then he'd showered quickly and spent the rest of the night—and part of the day—just holding Lynk in his arms while they slept. It still amazed him how the simple act had brought him so much contentment.

"It was nice. I haven't slept that well in a very, very long time. It's so easy to feel safe with you, though."

If Lynk didn't stop it, they'd be leaving the meeting early whether his smaller mate wanted to or not. The romantic in him felt all mushy at the declaration. The alpha in him, however, wanted to find the nearest flat surface and fuck Lynk into next week.

Lynk's hand settled on his upper thigh and squeezed as he tilted his head to the side, baring the side of his neck. The vein that snaked along the column of his throat pulsed with his heartbeat, and Kieran had to close his eyes and take several deep breaths to calm himself.

Leaning closer, he nipped at Lynk's earlobe and made that special part growl, part purr sound that his mate loved so much. "Be careful, baby. You're playing with fire."

"Maybe you should punish me," Lynk whispered back with a mischievous grin.

Remembering the things that Lynk considered punishment, Kieran tensed and leaned away. It had killed him every time his lover had asked him for those things. Even if Lynk enjoyed the pain, it still made Kieran's gut clench painfully.

He'd been young and impulsive those very long four hundred years ago. He hadn't understood what being in a relationship really meant, but he'd been so drawn to Lynk. It had felt as though his very soul would shrivel and die if they were separated. Which, from what he'd learned the night before, that was probably true.

His life back then had been a pampered one. His parents had money and were very generous with their only son. Never had he wanted for anything. Things had been a complete one-eighty this time around, and he'd had to grow up fast. Some days he felt much older than his thirty-four years.

Maybe he could find a compromise, a way to balance Lynk's needs with his own natural instinct to keep any harm from coming to his misguided lover. Lynk had once told him that the pain was the only thing that ever gave him peace. Well, Kieran was determined to change that. There had to be another way, and he'd figure it out for both of them.

"So, we're in agreement then?" Torren asked.

Shit! He'd completely missed what they were saying. Not that it really mattered. Someone would fill him in on the finer points after the meeting. Still, perhaps he should pay attention.

Well, everyone seemed to be in agreement for whatever the hell they were talking about. People were bobbing their heads or offering verbal concurrences. Raven was on his feet for some odd reason and seemed to have most of the group's attention.

"I've known Gideon for a long time. I'll feel him out and see what he knows without being too obvious."

Kieran had to suppress a snort at this. Raven wasn't exactly known for his subtlety. The history between him and the Snake River Enforcer was curious, however. Kieran made a mental note to badger the hell out of the vampire about it later. Raven would love that.

"Behave," Lynk whispered, but he was grinning like a Cheshire cat.

Having Lynk always rummaging around in his head would take some getting used to, but Kieran figured it wasn't such a bad thing. Since they could feel each other's emotions and listen in on private thoughts, it would be pointless to try to lie or hide things from one another. Not that he would do any such thing, but it was still nice that temptation had been removed from his path.

"I heard that," Lynk teased him.

The man was becoming increasingly more relaxed with him since revealing the skeletons in his closet. Once he realized that Kieran wasn't going to bolt, even though he now knew all of Lynk's dark and twisted secrets, he'd been dropping his defenses one shield at a time.

"Has Leader Tuesday contacted The Council about what happened yesterday?" Raina asked from where she sat beside Torren.

Kieran was so damn proud of her he could burst. His baby sister not only had a mate and babies of her own, but she was now an elder on The Council, using her brilliance to help bring peace to their world. He'd always known she was smart and fierce. It was amazing to see others recognizing it as well.

"No," Elder Cortez answered with a shake of his head. "That concerns me most of all. Anyone else would have been on the phone or our doorstep within minutes after the incident."

"Which makes it look like he has something to hide," Jory commented from Raina's other side.

Truth be known, Kieran was pretty damn proud of the little runt, too. He'd come to Haven with nothing—not even clothes on his back. It wasn't so long ago that he'd been scared of his own shadow and couldn't even talk to his mate, Stavion, without practically wetting himself. Now he had a seat on The Council, providing representation for the demons. All the changes that had taken place in Haven in the last year were a little surreal.

Scanning the crowd, Kieran found Stavion sitting in the front row, beaming up at Jory like he was the first rays of sunlight after a lifetime of darkness. Just beside him, Aslan was gazing at Torren in a similar fashion. All around the meeting room, different sets of mates were touching with a subtle intimacy or making goo-goo eyes at each other.

Three days ago, Kieran would have rolled his eyes and gagged at their lovesick actions. Now, looking down at his hand resting lightly on the inside of Lynk's thigh, the way they were leaning together, the simple fact that he couldn't stop sneaking looks at his mate, he had a feeling he had become the very thing he'd once mocked. Surprisingly, he couldn't bring himself to care.

He was happy, truly happy for the first time in his life. It wasn't faked or forced. He didn't have to plaster a smile on his face and play at being content. The feelings came easily, naturally now. It actually kind of scared the hell out of him considering how short a time he'd known Lynk, but then again, they had a *very* long history together.

"This…" Torren trailed off as he shuffled through some papers in front of him. "Zasha Gershwin. Has anyone heard a complaint from him? If I thought my mate was being kept from me, I'd be beating down someone's door and demanding to know why."

"No, love," Aslan said with a chuckle. "You'd be removing heads from shoulders."

"Same thing," Torren answered with an unconcerned wave of his hand. "My point is that it seems suspicious that he was so vehement in his claim to Lynk, yet he hasn't pursued him further."

When no one said anything else, Kieran squeezed Lynk's leg and stood. "We think it was a ploy to hold Lynk inside Snake River so they could question him about certain types of magic." He kept his response vague, unsure of how many in attendance knew about the Book of the Banished, or that Thane Braddock was being held in the coven.

Torren knew all of this, of course, but perhaps other members of The Council would have some further insight. If Zasha was truly mated to Thane as they had theorized, it was going to cause more problems than it solved, but at least it would help Kieran to rest easier. Just thinking about how the asshole had bitten Lynk made him want to run all the way to Snake River and rip the vampire's heart out with his bare hands. Probably not the best move for interspecies relations, but it would make him feel a hell of a lot better about the entire ordeal.

"Thank you for your discretion, Kieran, but I think everyone here knows about the Book of the Banished." Elder Layke Winters shifted in his chair and pushed his long, silver-blond hair behind his shoulder. "I'm not sure that I agree, however. Before you arrived, did Leader Tuesday have any indication that you would be bringing Lynk Braddock with you?"

Kieran looked across the aisle to Demos and Varik for answers. Since he'd kind of just tagged along instead of being invited, he had no idea what arrangements had been made.

"No," Varik answered with a frown. "I spoke with Zasha personally and informed him that Demos and I would be visiting with guests. I never said who those guests were."

"There you have it." Elder Camdin Maywater nodded slowly as he rubbed at his chin. It was his first Council meeting since being named representative to the fae. Kieran had never actually met him before, but he would have imagined a faerie to be small and petite like his friend, Kendall.

Camdin was easily the largest man in the room, and the place was crawling with big, brawny Enforcers. His voice was soft and musical, though, not the deep baritone Kieran had expected. The man was a complete mystery to him, and judging by the looks of confusion on most everyone else's faces, he wasn't alone.

"There would not have been sufficient time for Leader Tuesday to devise such an elaborate plan. I think Mr. Gershwin does believe Lynk to be his mate, so the question is why." Camdin cocked his head to the side and considered Lynk for a long time before he spoke again. "Whatever Leader Tuesday is planning—if anything—I don't believe Zasha Gershwin is in on it."

"So, what do we do?" Stavion wanted to know.

Torren looked down the row at his fellow elders and sighed. "We double the number of Enforcers patrolling the grounds. Raven will get in touch with whoever this Gideon person is, and Varik, I'm going to ask you to try and contact Zasha again."

"Someone should speak directly with Leader Tuesday."

Kieran groaned and settled back into his seat. He respected Stavion as a leader and a person, but he just didn't get why the man always felt the need to talk. Sometimes it was easier to get results by blowing shit up or kicking it to the ground. This seemed like one of those situations.

"Are you volunteering?" Jory asked with an arched eyebrow. He obviously didn't like the idea, but it was clear that he wouldn't argue or diminish Stavion's authority in front of the rest of The Council. He really was the perfect mate for the uptight vampire leader.

"I was thinking of someone unfamiliar to him and unassuming. Someone who won't intimidate or pose a threat to him."

"I'll do it."

Kieran chuckled under his breath when Galen rose to his feet. No way in hell was Bannon going to let him do something so foolish.

"No, ya bloody well won't!" Bannon shouted right on cue as he grabbed Galen around the waist and wrestled him back into his seat.

"Wait," Jory called and held up both hands. "He might be on to something." He rolled his eyes when Bannon growled at him. "I don't mean we're going to send him to Snake River by himself. What about the dreamwalking, though? Can you create a dreamscape where Leader Tuesday will feel relaxed enough that Galen can probe his thoughts? Maybe pull in Zasha, Gideon, and this other Enforcer, Axton, as well."

"That's actually a good idea," Torren agreed. "He won't be expecting it."

"Could we pull Thane into this dream, too?" Lynk stood and rested his hands on the bench in front of him. "If that's possible, I think I should go as well. I have the strongest connection to him."

"Well, if he's going, so am I." It was a good idea, and Kieran could admit that. He wouldn't stop Lynk from trying to help his brother, but he wanted to be there to watch over his mate in case things went wrong.

"It's the best way for Varik and Raven to contact their friends," Stavion added. "It would be much safer than a phone call."

All eyes turned to Bannon and Galen. "Can you do it?" Torren asked.

Bannon dipped his head. "It'll be a complicated dream world, but I can do it. I'll be needin' a day or two so I can work out the logistics."

The relief at finally having a workable plan was obvious in the faces of those in the room. Kieran was just happy that they wouldn't have to physically confront their enemies without having more information about them first.

"Thank you."

Kieran arched an eyebrow in question when Lynk settled down beside him on the bench. "Why are you thanking me?" And would this gratitude extend to them being naked? He wouldn't say that part out loud, though.

Lynk laughed quietly. "You are incorrigible. Thank you for not treating me like I'm weak or helpless." He paused and his grin turned wicked. "I'll thank you properly when we get home."

Kieran jumped up, grabbed Lynk's wrist, and pulled him toward the double doors at the back of the room. As far as he was concerned, the meeting was over.

"You *were* talking about the naked part, right?" He probably should have clarified that before dragging his mate along behind him like a Neanderthal, but most of his brain cells were now located in his dick.

Lynk's eyes lit up, and his nod was measured. "Yes, sir."

"How far is it back to the house?"

"I don't know. Six or seven minutes, maybe?"

Kieran grabbed Lynk around the waist, lifted him off his feet, and pressed his back against the wall in the long corridor. Then he crushed their mouths together while he slid his hand under the hem of his lover's shirt.

As hard as his dick was throbbing, that was entirely too long to wait.

Chapter Eleven

Lynk figured he should probably feel mortified at being mauled in such a public place, but all he could think was *yes, yes, yes!* Really, how was he supposed to think anything different with his mate's hands on him?

All during the meeting he'd been hit with wave after wave of Kieran's desire and bombarded with the man's lustful thoughts. His cock had been hard and his balls aching since they'd first stepped into the room. Every little touch or casual smile from his lover had only served to intensify everything that he was already feeling.

Kieran's tongue tangled with his, twisting, sliding, and caressing. His hands were everywhere, leaving Lynk's skin burning where he stroked or groped him. While Kieran had seemingly lost his mind, Lynk was in heaven—living in his every fantasy.

A strong alpha male had him pinned against the wall and wasn't shy about taking what he wanted. He was completely at Kieran's mercy, being dominated by a man who couldn't even wait through a car ride home before he had to have him. While some small voice worried about being caught, the larger, hedonistic part of him found that it made the episode all the more erotic.

Though Kieran was forceful and aggressive, he was still in control. What might appear as frenzied or frantic movements to others, Lynk knew each touch, each kiss, and every swivel of Kieran's hips was purposeful and calculated, designed to bring him as much pleasure as possible.

"Hands over your head." Kieran's voice was hoarse and rasping, dripping with arousal.

Lynk complied immediately, straightening his arms over his head and pressing his knuckles against the wall. Nimble fingers had the button of his jeans undone and his zipper down in record time, freeing his straining erection from its confinement.

Hissing in a breath through clenched teeth, Lynk closed his eyes and dropped his head forward when Kieran palmed his length and began to jerk him in a fast, steady rhythm. Lynk could have helped them along with a little magic. He *could* have removed their clothing. He *could* have slicked and stretched his hole, readying himself for Kieran's thick cock.

In the short time they'd been together, he'd discovered that his mate was adamantly against such things, though. They'd found their way together twice during the night, and each time Kieran had refused to let Lynk use his magic. Apparently he enjoyed the journey as much as he did the end prize, which was more than fine with Lynk. It made him feel special instead of like he was just a willing partner Kieran was using to get his kinks off.

In short order, Kieran had his own cock out, lining it up with Lynk's and fisting both in one hand. Lynk could feel Kieran's dick pulse, watched as a drop of pre-cum dripped down the side of the crown. He was enthralled, utterly fascinated by the single tear of clear moisture that smeared between their cocks as Kieran began to stroke them both at once.

The arm around his waist held him firmly in place, not allowing for even the tiniest of thrusts on his part. Not much was required of him but to sit back and enjoy the ride, so that was exactly what he did. His eyelids drifted closed again, and his head fell back against the sheetrock. The friction gliding up and down his shaft sent electrical waves up his spine and caused his skin to break out in gooseflesh.

Kieran grunted and panted against the side of his neck, his warm breath and soft lips creating a chain reaction in Lynk's body. His shoulders jerked, his muscles tensed, and his balls rolled inside his tight sac. His dick swelled inside Kieran's fist, and heat infused his cheeks while tingles raced out to his extremities.

"Please, sir," he begged as his lower abs clenched with his impending climax.

"Open your eyes, Lynk."

His eyelids snapped open, and he lifted his head to look at his lover.

"Put your arms around my neck."

Lynk shivered as he hurried to obey, his body burning with desire at the authority in Kieran's voice. Their foreheads rested together, their noses almost touched, and mere centimeters separated their mouths, but Kieran didn't kiss him like he'd expected.

"Tell me who you belong to, sugar."

"You, sir," Lynk panted, struggling to hold back his orgasm as Kieran jerked him harder and faster.

"You need me."

"Yes, sir." *More than you know.*

"More importantly, you *want* to need me."

He'd never really thought of it that way, but he couldn't deny the truth in the words. "Yes, sir."

Kieran closed his eyes and groaned as his hips jerked and his rhythm faltered. "Beg me, Lynk. Beg for what you want."

"Please, sir. I need to come. Please, can I come?"

Kieran groaned again, and his fist clenched around their shafts. "Then come for me, Lynk. Now." He twisted his wrist so that his fingers rubbed just under the ridge of Lynk's crown, and he slammed their mouths together in a demanding kiss that curled Lynk's toes right there inside his boots.

Music to his ears, the words released him from his self-imposed restraint, and Lynk erupted like a geyser, spraying heated seed from his slit and making a mess of both their shirts. Kieran followed swiftly, moaning into Lynk's mouth as cum blasted from his cock to swirl and mingle with Lynk's.

While he doubted he'd ever come so hard from a hand job, Lynk wanted more. His ass clenched greedily, wanting to be stretched and filled. His dick was still hard, still aching, needing more of Kieran's attention. The intense climax had done little to curb his craving for his lover. It might have even made the need stronger.

Kieran pulled his T-shirt off over his head and made a half-hearted attempt to clean them up. Multitasking obviously wasn't something he excelled at, however. Or maybe he was just much more interested in his exploration of Lynk's mouth. Whichever it was, by the time Kieran ended the kiss, neither of them was very clean, and Lynk was whimpering in frustration as his dick continued to throb.

"Six or seven minutes?" Kieran mumbled against his swollen lips.

"Give or take," Lynk returned, excitement flowing through him at the implications of the question.

Kieran dropped him to his feet and held him steady as he tried in vain to put their clothes back to rights. He finally gave up and just pulled Lynk along toward the exit with a growl. "I can make it in four."

* * * *

"Lean back against the door and push your pants off your hips." Kieran kept most of his attention of the road but snuck glances at Lynk out of the corner of his eye. Grabbing the travel-size bottle of lube from the cupholder, he tossed it at his mate, smirking when Lynk's eyes rounded and he clutched the tube like it was made of gold.

He hadn't been sure if he'd wanted to beat his brothers senseless or sing their praises when he'd found his pickup in the parking lot along with the bottle of lube and a note on the driver's seat telling him to enjoy his gift. Watching Lynk strip out of his boots and jeans then spread his legs so that one draped over the seatback, he was leaning toward the latter.

"Stroke your cock and finger your hole, but don't come." He fumbled with the button on his jeans so he could free his own straining dick and give it room to breathe before he caused himself serious damage.

"Yes, sir." Lynk slicked his fingers and wasted no time inserting two into his quivering entrance. His eyes locked on Kieran's weeping cock as he fisted his own shaft and pumped his hips up, sliding his rigid length through his tight grasp.

"See something you like?" Keeping a tight grip on the steering wheel and slowing his speed, Kieran slid two fingers under his cock and lifted it for Lynk's viewing pleasure.

Lynk sucked his bottom lip between his teeth and nodded.

"I can't hear you, sugar."

"Yes, sir. I like it very much." Both hands moved in tandem, plunging into his hole and flying over his cock. Perspiration beaded across his forehead, dampening his ebony hair so that it clung to his face, and his breathing came in great, panting gasps.

Lynk's feelings of lust slammed into Kieran like a tsunami while the cab of the pickup was permeated with the tantalizing scent of sex and carnal surrender. "Add another finger, sugar."

His mate extracted both fingers, added a third, and pushed all three into his clenching channel. The strain on his handsome face was evident as his eyes squeezed closed and the cords in his neck strained—his mouth open in a silent scream. Liberal amounts of pre-cum leaked from the tip of his cock, covering the crown so that it glistened in the moonlight filtering through the windows.

Lynk's back bowed, his hips bucked upward, and Kieran could see his heart pulsing in the vein in his throat. He'd barely even touched himself, and already Kieran felt his orgasm building just from watching his lover pleasure himself. Crap, why weren't they there yet? Had he missed a turn somewhere?

"Just past that row of trees." Lynk answered his unspoken question through strangled moans.

As promised, the long driveway appeared on the left within seconds. Pulling onto the drive just so he was off the main road, Kieran slammed on the brake and threw the pickup into park. Shoving the seat back as far as it would go, he snatched the lube up from the seat where Lynk had abandoned the bottle and used it to slick his aching cock.

"Come here," he ordered, holding his shaft upright by the base.

Lynk was out of his seat and crawling into Kieran's lap in the next blink. He didn't wait for permission or command, either. Straddling Kieran's thighs, Lynk sank over him, impaling himself until Kieran's cock was encased to the root inside the tightest, most amazing heat.

"Oh, fuck," he groaned, dropping his head back on the seat and thrusting up as he dug his fingers into the naked flesh on Lynk's hips.

"That's the idea." Lynk mouthed the side of Kieran's throat as he rose and fell, dropping hard into Kieran's lap over and over. "Please, sir. More, I need more." He insinuated a hand between them, reaching for his shaft where it rubbed against Kieran's abs.

"No. Hands on the seat behind me."

Lynk whimpered, but did as he was told, pressing both palms flat against the seat on either side of Kieran's shoulders. "I'm all that you need, Lynk. Do you understand?"

"Yes, sir."

Kieran snapped his hips, pulling Lynk down on his cock with every forceful plunge. The truck rocked with their movements. The windows fogged with their rapid breathing while an inferno raged though Kieran's body.

"I need...I need..." Lynk rested his temple against the side of Kieran's head and groaned as his whole body shuddered, clearly on the verge of climax.

"You need me."

"Yes," Lynk hissed. "I need you."

Kieran trailed his tongue over the salty skin on his lover's shoulder. "Then come for me, sugar. Strangle my cock. Make me feel it." He licked again before he struck, sinking his canines into the damp flesh while his arms locked around Lynk's waist like steel bands.

His mate screamed loud enough to make his eardrums hurt as he exploded, his cock spurting and his inner walls convulsing around Kieran, massaging his cock, milking him. "Come for me, love," Lynk rasped, grinding himself against Kieran's groin.

The orgasm that rippled through him stole the breath from his lungs and left him momentarily deaf and blind. His growl was loud enough to vibrate the windows as he filled Lynk to the brim, overflowing his snug channel with his seed.

"Damn, it just keeps getting better," Kieran said hoarsely when speech finally returned to him. "You okay, sugar?" He skimmed his palm down Lynk's spine and peppered kisses over the side of his face.

Lynk snuggled against his chest while his body shuddered with aftershocks. His arms looped around Kieran's neck, holding on to him tightly. "Better than okay."

A movement outside the window caught Kieran's attention just before a large fist pounded against the glass. "Man, you're blocking the drive!"

Wiping away the fog, Kieran kept his other arm around Lynk and smiled up at the man's brother. "Hi, Torren."

Torren snorted and rolled his eyes. "Get a room. That's my baby brother, you know. I really don't need to see this."

"Then close your eyes or go away," Lynk said, making no attempt to remove himself from Kieran's lap.

"Just move the damn truck." Then the eldest Braddock stomped away, presumably to his own vehicle parked right behind them.

Kieran and Lynk fell together in laughter, and Kieran suddenly felt like a teenager being caught in the backseat of his car by his partner's father. Instead of being afraid for his life, though, he found the entire situation hilarious.

Gods, life with Lynk was so much better than anything he'd experienced on his own. He'd do whatever it took to never lose that feeling. He'd been too young and stupid to hold on to it before, but he wouldn't let it slip through his hands again.

Chapter Twelve

"What do you mean I can't go?" Lynk fisted his hands on his hips and snarled at his brother and his mate. For two days he'd been waiting for Bannon to come up with a suitable dream sequence that would allow them to extract the information they needed to save Thane. Now that everything was in place, Torren and Kieran were telling him that he wasn't going to help.

"It's too dangerous," Kieran said. Lynk was sure he was going for soothing and coaxing, but it wasn't working.

"Besides that," Torren interrupted, "your presence could hurt more than help. All it would take is for Zasha or Leader Tuesday to recognize you, and the whole thing is blown. That's my final decision, and I'm not backing down from it."

"What about disguising us? I thought you said that Bannon could do that." He jabbed a finger in Kieran's direction. "And why does he get to go? You don't think they'll recognize him?"

When neither man had a ready answer, Lynk found his suspicion piqued. They were hiding something from him. More importantly, *Kieran* was keeping secrets.

"Lynk, you're not going," Kieran insisted, dropping all pretenses of the supportive lover. "I would lose my goddamn mind if anything happened to you. Please don't argue with me on this one."

"We just got you back," Torren added, his face somber. "I want to rescue Thane as much as you do, but don't make me choose between the two of you. I won't sacrifice one brother to save the other. Don't ask me to do that."

They weren't playing fair. Lynk wasn't asking them to sacrifice anything. He might not be the almighty Torren, but he was damn powerful, and he could help. Why didn't anyone ever believe in him? He'd thought Kieran did, but he now understood how wrong he'd been.

Unless... "What happened?"

"Nothing," Kieran answered a little too quickly. He suddenly found a spot on the arm of the sofa to be very interesting.

"You were in full support of me doing this as long as you could be at my side." Lynk rose from the armchair and prowled toward his mate. "You didn't think it was too dangerous or that I was too weak two days ago. Tell me what changed."

"I was just trying to pacify you." Kieran still wouldn't look at him. "I didn't want to cause a scene at the meeting."

Lie. Lynk could practically smell the untruth rolling off his lover. "Wow, and I thought Torren was a bad liar."

"Am not," Torren mumbled under his breath without a shred of conviction.

Well, two could play at that game. Or was it three? Whatever. "Fine. When is Bannon supposed to be here?"

"Tomorrow at five," Kieran answered. "We have to wait for all the vamps to be sleeping for the day. Raven and Varik will be here before the sun comes up and hang out in the basement until it's time."

"And you're not going to tell me what happened that suddenly changed everything, are you?"

"No."

Well, at least he wasn't lying anymore. "Okay, well if you really think that it's too dangerous for me..." Lynk trailed off and shrugged. "I'm going to bed. Are you coming?"

"That's it? That's all you're going to say?" Kieran's eyebrows drew together, and he sounded incredulous to say the least.

"What would you like me to say? It's obvious that I'm not going to budge you on this, so what's the point in arguing?" Lynk lifted his right hand and waved it in front of him. Kieran's clothes disappeared. "I mean what could I possibly do to help?"

"Hey!"

Lynk snapped his fingers, binding Kieran to the sofa so that only his eyes and lips could move. "Obviously I'm far too weak to participate in such a dangerous endeavor."

"Lynk Braddock, I swear to everything that is holy, if you don't—"

He snapped his fingers again, effectively cutting off Kieran's threat. "You'll do what exactly?" True, he needed Kieran's strength. He melted under the man's dominance. The silence from his whirlwind of thoughts could only be brought about by what his mate could give him.

That didn't mean that he was going to roll over and expose his belly when people he loved were in danger, though. Kieran might have several inches and nearly forty pounds on him, but when it came down to logistics, Lynk would always win. He wasn't a child. He wasn't helpless. And they were going to damn sure stop treating him as such.

"Lynk, this isn't going to help," Torren admonished, though he looked to be having a hard time keeping a straight face.

Very well then. Lynk waved a hand toward his brother, stripping Torren, and mumbled under his breath. All at once, Torren flew backward, pinned to the wall and splayed out with his hands over his head. "You were saying?"

"You know I'm stronger than you." Torren's muscles bunched as he strained against his invisible bonds.

"Prove it."

His brother smiled wickedly, and the next thing Lynk knew he was curled into a pretzel on the floor with his feet behind his head. *So undignified.*

Kieran shook with laughter, though he was still unable to open his lips. His amusement at Lynk's predicament was less than endearing. It was just Lynk's luck that Aslan chose that moment to walk into the room. Torren's mate stopped dead in his tracks, cocked his head to the side, and arched an eyebrow.

"What are you doing?" he asked casually, addressing Torren as though nothing unusual was happening.

"Lynk started it."

Aslan snorted. "Right. That's why he looks like he's trying to shove his head up his own ass." He turned his attention to Kieran. "Is he going to be okay? He looks like he's about to have a stroke."

Lynk wiggled around like a turtle that had been flipped on his shell so that he could get a better look at his lover. That poor guy looked like he was about to burst with his face almost purple from having to hold in his laughter. Deciding to take pity on him, Lynk released his gag spell. Once freed, Kieran roared with laughter, his whole body vibrating with it.

Still locked in the embarrassing and uncomfortable position, Lynk suddenly found himself levitating off the floor until he hovered two feet or so from the carpet. He only had a second to glare at his brother before he started spinning in circles so fast that he thought he was going to puke as the room whizzed by him in a blur.

"Okay!" he finally shouted. "I give!"

Torren didn't let up, though. Faster and faster he spun, sometimes even somersaulting in the air until it felt like his brain was going to explode out of the top of his skull and his stomach lodged in his throat. Unfortunately, he knew from past experience that Torren wouldn't stop until Lynk either vomited or passed out. It had been Torren's favorite way to torture him when they were kids.

His mate's laughter came to abrupt halt, and he was off the sofa and snarling in Torren's face before Lynk even registered what was happening. "Put him down."

Heedless of the warning in Kieran's tone, Torren chuckled and sent Lynk tumbling through the air around the room. It was in that moment that Kieran did the worst possible thing he could have done.

He wrapped his fingers around Torren's neck and squeezed, breaking the witch's concentration.

Lynk stopped spinning and fell onto the coffee table like a ton of bricks, snapping it as though it was made of nothing more than cardboard, and causing him to cry out in pain. Abandoning his hold on Torren, Kieran flew to his side, his hands hovering over Lynk, obviously not sure where or *if* to touch him.

"Oh, shit. Lynk, talk to me. Are you okay? Where does it hurt, sugar?"

"Everywhere." The room was still spinning, and he felt like the table wasn't the only thing broken. "This is so your fault."

"Yes," Kieran replied solemnly. "It is. I'm sorry. I'll tell you anything you want to know. You can come with us into Bannon's dream. Whatever you want."

It wasn't how he'd planned to gain his mate's acquiescence. Surely there could have been a less painful way. Still, it accomplished what he'd set out to do. Only, he'd wanted to prove he could handle himself, not have Kieran fawn all over him because he'd ended up getting his ass handed to him by his big brother. "You're naked." It was so very hard for Lynk to think coherently with his mate hovering over him, gloriously bare and smelling so wonderful.

"And whose fault is that?" Kieran arched an eyebrow at him, though he was smiling that special, confident smile that always turned Lynk into putty.

"Oh, right. *Revelabit.*" Instantly, Kieran's clothes reappeared, though Lynk was a bit sorry to see all of that smooth, tanned skin go. It wasn't like he didn't have access to it whenever he wanted, though. Kieran would never deny him, always viewing them as equals.

That thought alone went a long way in soothing his agitation over Kieran's secret keeping. Whatever his mate was hiding, he did it to protect Lynk, not because he thought Lynk was weak, but because that was what people did when they loved someone. They went to any lengths to protect them—even from themselves.

"Can you move?"

The pain had already begun to subside, and he didn't feel quite so queasy any longer. Lynk wiggled his toes and fingers experimentally and rocked his head from side to side on his neck. Nothing felt broken. "I'm okay. I'll probably be a little sore tomorrow, but everything is where it should be."

"C'mon, Lynk." Kieran helped him up and lifted him into his arms. "A nice, hot bath should help, and we'll see if Elder Jackass can rustle up some pain meds."

"Maybe you could release said elder from the wall first," Torren snapped, still struggling against the fastening spell Lynk had placed on him.

Aslan looked like he was going to rupture something from laughing so hard. "Will he eventually get free without you?"

"He could get free now if he was really concentrating on it." Lynk had no illusions about being more powerful than his brother. Snuggled in Kieran's arms, he wasn't too fussed about it, either.

"In that case, go on and have that bath." Aslan stopped laughing and gave Torren a seductive smirk. "I'll take good care of him."

Torren stopped struggling, and he stared his mate up and down, practically undressing him with his eyes. "Get out," he ordered, without even looking in Lynk's direction.

The look of lust in his eyes was enough to make Lynk shudder. "Let's go. This is definitely not something that I want to see."

"Not to worry." Kieran dropped a kiss on the top of his head as he carried him out of the room. "We'll find a little privacy and make our own magic."

* * * *

He'd only wanted to prevent Lynk from getting hurt. Instead, just the opposite had happened. While it had been nothing more than sibling bickering, it could have been so much worse.

Placing his lover gently on the bed, Kieran brushed his lips against Lynk's and smiled. "I'll start the bath."

Lynk didn't return his smile, though. "What happened? Are you ever going to tell me?"

Sighing in resignation, Kieran stretched out on the mattress beside his mate, realizing that a soak in the tub would have to be postponed for less enjoyable pursuits. "Zasha has requested a formal hearing with The Council. He's protesting our mating, and requesting the right to challenge me."

"Challenge you for the right to claim me as a mate?" Lynk shot up so quickly that their foreheads smacked together. Heedless of the injury, Lynk just shook his head as though flinging off water and gaped at Kieran. "You can't be serious! He can't do that. Can he do that? You've already claimed me. Zasha is not my mate!"

"Hush now." Kieran stroked the side of Lynk's face, tucking his hair back behind his ear. "I know, sugar. I know. Torren doesn't have a choice but to grant him the hearing, though. Plus, Zasha has Leader Tuesday backing him."

"What's going to happen at this meeting?"

"I don't know. If Zasha argues his case convincingly, I assume that The Council will be forced to grant him the right to challenge me." Kieran wished he had better answers, but in truth, he didn't know what to expect in the days to come.

"When is the hearing?"

Kieran flinched. "Uh, tomorrow evening."

"Crackerjacks!" Lynk grumbled a few more pseudo-curses under his breath before regaining control. "So, we only get one shot at this dream thing. If we don't learn anything useful, we're screwed at the hearing."

"There's also the chance that we can find out about Thane, but nothing that will help us with Zasha."

Kieran chuckled when his mate growled at him. "Thank you so much for the optimistic spin on our predicament. It's very helpful. Is there anything we can do to circumvent this challenge?"

"If Bannon can't help us find out anything useful, then we can try to prove our case." Kieran was the one to growl this time. He didn't like the idea at all. It left Lynk too exposed, too vulnerable, and he wouldn't be close enough to protect him if something happened.

On the other hand, in his shifted form on the full moon, there was absolutely nothing that would prevent him from getting to his mate. No matter where Lynk was, no matter how far away or what obstacles presented themselves in his path, Kieran would find him.

"Won't that mean that Zasha will also be able to provide evidence to prove that I'm *his* mate? How does that work? How do you know for sure with vampires? And why doesn't anyone care what I want?"

They were all good questions, but unfortunately, Kieran didn't have a response. "I care what you want, Lynk, but I don't know all the rules. I don't understand anything about politics, especially vampire politics." He pushed his lover back to the mattress and pinned him there by his shoulders while he loomed over him. "I promise you this, though. No matter what happens or what those idiots on The Council say, I won't let anyone take you away from me. You got that?"

"Same goes for you," Lynk answered firmly. "I don't care what they say. You are my mate, and I've waited a long time to get you back. I'm not about to let you go now."

To know Lynk would fight so vehemently for him—for them—sent a wave of warmth flowing from Kieran's chest and out to his extremities. He really should have known better than to doubt Lynk's feelings for him, though. The man had faced down a group of angry vampires for him. If that wasn't proof enough that Lynk wanted him, he didn't know what was.

"We'll figure this out. No one is going anywhere. Though, it might be a hell of a lot easier if we can find Thane. If Torren's theory about him being Zasha's mate is right, it could save a lot of trouble and stress."

"I would like nothing better, but how do you propose that we find my wayward brother?"

Kieran couldn't stop himself from smiling. Gods, he loved the way Lynk talked sometimes, like hints of his old lives were sneaking into his speech. What he loved even more was peeling away that layer of formality and reducing the man to a babbling, writhing, lust-filled mess. There was never any telling what would come out of Lynk's mouth when he was in the throes of passion. It was adorable, if also a bit humorous.

"I guess we start with Bannon."

"Why didn't you just tell me? I'm not so fragile, Kieran."

He knew that. Once the summons for a formal hearing had come in, he'd lost his mind just a little. The only thought that filtered through the anger was shielding Lynk from anyone who wanted to tear them apart. "I guess I panicked. I don't want you to have to worry about these kinds of things. That's what I'm here for. That's my job."

"That's very sweet in an odd sort of way. I can handle this, Kieran. I've fought bad guys before. I even have a cape and everything."

It took a second for Kieran to realize that Lynk had made a joke. It was so out of character for him that Kieran was stunned silent for another moment before he broke up into laughter. "You're a real superhero, huh?"

Lynk's demeanor became serious as his arms lifted to wind around Kieran's neck. "Sometimes I need you to make everything disappear. Sometimes I need to give you that control and let you make the decisions for me. I always crave your dominance. Those dynamics will never change, but I'm not the same person as I was in our former life. Much the same as you are a very different person than before—all while being the same man I fell in love with at the core."

"I understand that, and I feel the same way. I love the things I remember about our life together, but I'm enjoying getting to know the person you are now." The point to this discussion was still eluding him, however. "What are you trying to say?"

"That I don't need you to take care of me all the time," Lynk whispered. "Sometimes, I need to take care of you as well. I'm not a damsel in distress or a child afraid of the monster under his bed. I might not like confrontation, but I know how to fight my own battles, to fight for the people I love, and this time, I need you to let me do that."

"So, what you're trying to say is that I should stop coddling you and believe in you to make the right choices for what is best." Kieran dipped his head once. "I can do that." It wouldn't be easy. His natural instinct to charge in and save the day would always be there, but Lynk was right.

It didn't mean he had to like it, but the sexy smile and heated kiss his mate bestowed on him made it just a little easier to share some of the burden that lay before them.

Chapter Thirteen

"This is really the best disguise you could come up with?" Lynk stared down at his clothing in disgust and rubbed at the scraggly beard that adorned his chin and cheeks. He looked like a vagrant. His trousers were dirty and ripped. The shirt he assumed was meant to be white was more yellow than anything with a spot near his belly button that looked like…"Is that blood?"

"You're still gorgeous," Kieran assured him with a soft kiss behind Lynk's ear.

Lynk didn't know how the man could even stand to touch him, let alone kiss him. His hair was greasy and matted, his skin crawled with all the grime that coated it, and he smelled like something that belonged in a barn. "This is disgusting."

Bannon, Galen, Raven, and Varik all looked exactly the same as they normally did. Torren's normally black hair was now platinum blond, and his facial features were a bit sharper. It wasn't much of a disguise, but Lynk admitted that he wouldn't have recognized his brother if he didn't already know it was Torren.

Kieran, however, was dressed from head to foot in solid black. His gorgeous dark hair now flowed past his shoulders and was dyed the most shocking color of electric blue. Eyeliner along the bottom lids made him look dangerous rather than feminine. It all combined to form one erotic image of temptation that Lynk was having a hard time resisting. Who knew he'd be into such things?

"You are stunning," he breathed, his mouth going dry and his cock threatening to swell inside his shabby slacks.

Kieran gave him a shit-eating grin and jerked on the hem of his leather jacket. "You like?"

A throat clearing interrupted them before Lynk could embarrass himself, which he was immensely grateful for. "We need to be gettin' started now," Bannon said in his smooth Irish accent.

"So, how do we do this?" Varik asked casually as though he did this type of thing every day.

"We'll be hosting a party," Galen answered, obviously familiar with how his mate operated. "Bannon can populate the dream with enough people to keep everyone distracted long enough for you to speak with who you need and gather whatever information you can get."

"By bringing most of Snake River into this dreamscape, we're hoping that it will put Tuesday at ease and not arouse suspicion," Torren added. "If he was dreaming of a party, it would only make sense that it would include members of his own coven."

Yes, it all made perfect sense other than why Lynk needed to look and smell like a hobo. "You don't think a homeless man at this extravagant party will be somewhat of a red flag?"

"It's a block party." Bannon winked at him. "Just park yourself against a wall, and people, they'll be ignorin' ya. It'll make it easier to do your job without bein' interrupted." He didn't wait for a response as he turned away from Lynk, took Galen's hand, and closed his eyes.

"We can do this," Kieran whispered in his ear. "Just find Thane." A chaste kiss was dropped on Lynk's lips before Kieran backed away, moving farther across the enormous, vacant field.

The rolling fog, dark shadows, and ghostly beams cast by the moon were starting to creep him out. It was far too silent, as though all noise in the universe had been muted before passing through the thick, gray clouds that hovered around them.

A large building suddenly appeared out of nowhere right behind him, rising up out of the ground as though sprouted from a seed. Lynk gasped and backed away, staring around him with his mouth hanging open. More buildings appeared, along with bright lights as well as soft twinkling string lights. The volume inside their little world suddenly exploded into loud, thumping music, raucous laughter, and animated conversation.

There were people everywhere—some with drinks in their hands, others just standing together in small groups, smiling, chatting, and looking very pleased to be just where they were. Not one person appeared confused or suspicious about suddenly finding themselves thrown into a party where they hadn't been just moments before. The power of dreams was a magical thing.

Lynk didn't see any of his cohorts, though. They'd all dispersed into the crowd, leaving him very much on his own. A little quiver of panic worked its way up his spine, but he batted it away and prepared himself for what needed to be done. He didn't know how long they'd have, so he needed to make the most of his allotted time.

Settling himself against the wall of the brick building behind him, he slid down to the concrete sidewalk and tried to appear as unassuming as possible. A bottle of cheap whiskey appeared in his right hand, the cap removed, and only half-full of its contents. Lynk stared at it for a moment before snorting and rolling his eyes. Bannon Murphy was just a barrel of laughs—the idiot.

Curling the bottle close to his chest, Lynk figured he might as well play the part of drunken vagabond. So, he splayed his legs out in front of him, let his head loll to the side so that his ear rested on his shoulder, and hiccupped a couple of times just for effect.

Internally, he emptied his mind of all thoughts, shut out the noise around him, and dropped his shields—opening himself to his lost brother. *"Thane? Are you here?"*

"Hello, brother." Thane sounded weak, his voice muffled like he was speaking through a ball of cotton. *"It's been a long time."*

"We're going to help you. We'll get you out of there, but I need to know where you are. Is Leader Tuesday holding you in Snake River? Are you locked away in a dungeon somewhere?"

Lynk heard his brother snort at him through their mental bond. *"A dungeon? Perhaps he has me guarded by a dragon as well? The lonely and frightened damsel, forced to lament the loss of her freedom until the white knight arrives on his valiant steed to scale the castle walls."*

"Okay, now you're just being a dick." Lynk rolled his eyes. Thane had always been a bit theatrical and dramatic.

His rich, warm laughter traveled through their link, growing louder and more defined. *"Sorry, Lynk. It's just so much fun to tease you, though."*

"Yes, so you have all told me on numerous occasions. That's not helpful right now, though. I need to know where you are if we're going to get you out."

"I'm right here, of course."

"Thane!" It took a great deal of restraint for Lynk to remain seated and not throw himself at his twin. To outsiders, it would appear as though they weren't even related, let alone had shared the same womb.

Where he was small and thin, Thane was over six feet with muscles for days. His hair was a golden blond like sunshine on a wheat field, a stark contrast to Lynk's midnight locks. Thane's hair was longer than when Lynk had last seen him, and he was in desperate need of a shave.

"You look like shit," Thane commented with a wink as he settled on the ground beside Lynk. "Where are we anyway?"

"One of our Enforcers is a dream builder. And my appearance is a ruse. What's your excuse?"

"I've been held hostage for the last two years? I spent the last few months of that captivity inside a well? Are those good enough excuses for you?" Thane didn't sound bitter. In fact, there was a bit of amusement in his tone.

Lynk was horrified, however. "Where? In Snake River? Did Leader Tuesday do it? Are there guards? Why can't you use your magic to get out? What do they want with you?"

Thane chuckled under his breath. "Calm down, Lynk." The smile slid from his face, and he became serious. "You know exactly what they want, but I won't tell them where the Book of the Banished is. That's why they dropped me in the well. They're getting desperate and trying to crack me. I'm being held by vampires, but I don't know their names or even where I am. Snake River? Where exactly is that?"

"In Wyoming," Lynk supplied then shut his trap so that Thane could continue.

"Hmm." Thane scratched at the scraggly beard on his jaw, the hairs a shade darker than the sandy locks that fell from his crown to brush over the tops of his shoulders. "I'm not sure how I got all the way to Wyoming. I was in Belgium when they took me."

Lynk didn't know what to do with that bit of information, so he tucked it away to discuss with the others later. "How are they keeping you there?"

"They kept me sedated for the first few months. Now, they feed me only enough to keep me alive so that they can drink from me or syphon blood into vials. I think my magic is dying along with my body. It has abandoned me." He sounded so sad, almost ashamed of the things that had been done to him.

Looking his brother over with a critical eye, Lynk realized that Thane appeared pale, and his body mass was greatly reduced from the man he remembered. Still, he seemed larger than life to Lynk, who had always looked up to his twin, both literally and figuratively.

A fierce protectiveness filled him, reversing the positions they'd fallen into as children. The bigger and stronger twin, Thane, had accepted the role of Lynk's protector and never complained about the task, even taking Lynk's side against their other siblings. Now, however, it was Lynk who would be Thane's champion, a job he took very seriously.

"I'm going to get you out of that well. Be strong for just a little while longer, okay?"

Thane pressed his forefinger right between Lynk's eyes and asserted pressure. "What is going on inside here? What trouble have you gotten yourself into?"

Lynk frowned. "Who said I'm in trouble?"

"You are a horrible liar. I think it's probably a Braddock trait. Either way, I know something is going on, so you might as well spill it."

"There is a vampire named Zasha who thinks I'm his mate."

"But you're not."

"Correct. I have a mate. A big, possessive werewolf mate who is going to end up eating this vampire for desert if we don't get this sorted soon." If Zasha came anywhere near him, Lynk had little doubt that Kieran would react quite violently.

Thane whistled low. "A werewolf, you say? Well done, my brother." He winked roguishly and crossed his arms over his chest. "Why does this vampire think you belong to him?"

"I have a theory." Lynk bit his lip and looked away, unsure of how much to reveal. If Thane knew he had a mate out there waiting for him, his *Infinity* of all people, maybe it would give him more reason to fight for his life and freedom. Or it could completely backfire and blow up in Lynk's face.

"Just tell." Thane huffed in obvious exasperation. "I'm going to get it out of you eventually, so just save us both the time and trouble."

"I think Zasha may be your mate," Lynk blurted, watching Thane intently for his reaction. "When we were in Snake River a few days ago, I was searching for you through our bond. I was open to your energy. I think maybe Zasha is confused."

"A vampire mate," Thane mused with a crooked smile. "Is he here?"

Well, that wasn't the reaction Lynk had been expecting, but he supposed it was better than Thane getting pissed because he was being kept from his fated mate—a mate he could have been missing for hundreds of years now. "He's supposed to be here, but I really don't know where anyone is. They've all kind of scattered." Lynk flapped his hand around in front of him, indicating the party in full swing around them.

"What about this mate of yours? Can you get a lock on him?"

Lynk beamed. "Oh, yeah. Hold please." He closed his eyes and pushed his thoughts toward his lover, searching him out in the throng of people.

"Hey, sugar. Did you find Thane?"

"Of course. Do you know where Zasha is?"

"Nope, but our time is about up. Be ready to leave in three minutes or so."

"I have to go," Lynk said aloud to his brother. He embraced Thane, squeezing him hard before jumping to his feet. "We're coming for you. Don't give up yet."

Thane smiled, slow and easy as though he didn't have a care in the world. "I'll wait right where I am. Oh, and try to keep your werewolf from eating my mate before I have a chance to meet him."

"You are such an idiot." Still, Lynk couldn't help but laugh at his brother. "I'll do my best. Do you really think I'm right and Zasha is your mate?"

"I've rarely known you to be wrong about anything, so yes. I think Zasha is my mate." Thane tilted his head to the side and rubbed at his chin. "Have you tried explaining it to him? You might just gain an ally if you can convince him."

"This all hangs on the fact that he actually believes me to be his mate. There is the possibility that he's only acting on orders in an attempt to separate me from everyone and hold me in Snake River."

"You won't know unless you try. Not everyone is your enemy, Lynk."

Lynk frowned, shook his head, and walked backward as he noticed the dream beginning to collapse around him. "That doesn't make everyone my friend, either. Guilty until proven innocent."

* * * *

"Okay, so what do we know?" Torren asked as they all gathered in one of the rooms in the basement after waking up from their drug-induced sleep. With Varik and Raven joining their group, it was the only place in the house they could meet that was light-tight and allowed their friends the protection from the sun's harmful rays.

What had felt like only minutes to Kieran had actually been nearly two hours. He'd always thought it was exactly the opposite. A few minutes in the real world equaled several hours in a dream. It was a little disconcerting to have all of his preconceived notions proven false.

"I never saw Leader Tuesday," he offered when no one else spoke up. "Did anyone else?"

Everyone shook their heads with identical frowns on their faces. "I recognized a lot of people as members of the Snake River Coven, but I didn't see their infamous leader," Raven agreed. "I was, however, able to speak to Gideon."

"Did he put my brother in the well?"

All heads turned and every set of eyes in the room landed on Lynk. He didn't flinch or cower under their scrutiny, though. The look of anger and determination that shone on his face was sexy and provocative. It wasn't often that he asserted himself, but when he did, it always left Kieran in a state of high arousal.

"Thane is in a well?"

Lynk spared him a glance, his eyes softening just a bit at the corners before the mask fell over his face once more, and he faced down the rest of the room. "Thane said he's being imprisoned inside a well, but he doesn't know who's holding him. He also said that he was abducted while in Belgium then brought here to Wyoming about two years ago."

"What else did he say?" Torren looked anxious for the information, an expression not common to the elder's visage.

Lynk dropped his chin to his chest and sighed. "He thinks we should try to get Zasha on our side. If we can convince Zasha that it is really Thane who is his mate, then he'll want to do whatever he can to find him. That is Thane's theory anyway." He finally lifted his head and stared across the distance at Torren. "I don't know what to think or who to trust."

"We don't trust anyone until they prove otherwise." Kieran wasn't about to gamble Lynk's safety on a hunch. Unless someone had some solid evidence to persuade him otherwise, Zasha was still the enemy.

Torren studied him for a moment and dipped in his head in what Kieran assumed was agreement. Then he clasped his hands behind his back and turned to Raven. "What did Gideon say?"

"Not much. He did apologize about the whole fiasco with Lynk and Zasha, though. It makes me think that if something is going on in Snake River, Gideon isn't in on it. I've known him for a long time, and I'm confident that I could tell if he was lying."

It was still hearsay and not nearly good enough for Kieran. Settling against the wall at his back, he wound his arm around Lynk's shoulders and pulled him closer to his side. It wasn't sexual in nature, but he needed the physical contact with his mate. Maybe if he held on tight enough, he could shield the man from the entire world.

"What about Zasha?" Galen asked while everyone's focus turned to Varik. "Did you get anything out of him?"

"He insists that Lynk is his mate." Varik huffed out a sigh and shook his head. "He was pretty fucking adamant about it, too. If he's acting, he's damn good at it. So good, in fact, that he should probably pack his bags and head to Hollywood."

The vampire looked exhausted. His normally pale skin was almost gray. The dark circles under his eyes stood out in sharp relief, and he looked to be having trouble holding his head up. Raven didn't look in any better shape, and Kieran realized that being up during the day was taking its toll on the men.

"So, we're still exactly where we started." Torren's growl rolled up from his chest and bounced off the walls in the room. "Basically, we have dick."

"Well, we have a more precise location of where Thane is," Lynk responded reasonably. "I wouldn't say that it was a total waste."

No, but Kieran wouldn't call their excursion a success, either. While they continued to discuss the events of the dream and analyze different conversations, a shiver worked up his spine, signaling the descent of the sun toward the western horizon. He might only be forced to shift on the full moon, but he was still connected to the lunar goddess during the rest of the month.

Maybe it was time to face their troubles head-on. What was the worst that could happen by openly accusing Leader Tuesday of kidnapping and imprisoning a fellow paranormal?

Kieran frowned and hugged Lynk even tighter. Knowing his luck, the sky would fall or something equally as horrible would happen. Still, it wasn't like they were getting anywhere by beating around the bush and playing it cool.

If Leader Tuesday knew nothing about Thane's capture, he could prove to be a powerful ally. If he was behind it all…well, things couldn't get much worse than they already were. Right?

Chapter Fourteen

"You have to calm down," Kieran whispered out of the corner of his mouth. Lynk was vibrating so violently with his nerves that it shook Kieran's thigh where their legs were pressed together on the wooden bench inside The Council meeting hall.

"I'm trying," Lynk shot back.

Turning to his mate, Kieran grasped the witch's chin and squeezed, forcing Lynk's head up so that their eyes met. "Quiet," he ordered, though not harshly. "Everything will be fine. I've already told you that I'm not letting anyone take you away from me." He leaned closer until their noses almost touched and let the authority drip from his tone. "Quiet, sugar."

Lynk calmed at once, the trembling subsided, and his muscles relaxed until he was sagging against Kieran's side. "Thank you," he mumbled.

Wrapping his lover up close to him, Kieran kissed the top of his head and sighed. "We're going to be fine," he responded for what felt like the millionth time. He still wasn't sure if he believed it, but he had to hang on to that little bit of hope.

"Please state your name for The Council." Torren spoke casually, but his eyes glinted with malice and anger as he stared down from the dais at Zasha.

The vampire moved to the center of the small area just beyond the benches, halfway between the elders and those gathered behind him. "Zasha Aleric Gershwin, member of the Snake River Coven."

"Mr. Gershwin," Elder Cortez began with his faintly accented voice, "can you please inform the members of this gathering why you are here?"

Zasha stood straight and proud, his hands linked in front of him and his shoulders pushed back. "The werewolf Enforcer, Kieran Delaney, has claimed what is rightfully mine. Lynk Braddock is my true mate, and as such, I wish to file a formal complaint against Mr. Delaney for being in violation of one of our most sacred laws. If he refuses to relinquish his claim to Lynk, I ask permission from The Council to challenge him—as is my right."

There were several hisses and snarls that rolled through the crowd at his longwinded declaration. It was damn nice to see so many people on their side. Hell, he'd treated the new Moonlighter, Xander, like a freaking leper, and still the man was there to support him.

Surprisingly, it was his sister, Raina, who he felt most sorry for. It was her job as elder representative of the werewolves to be impartial and fair. When one of the members on trial happened to be her big brother, he imagined it wasn't an easy task for her.

She looked resolute, though, and Kieran's chest swelled with pride. Whatever happened, even if she ruled against him, he wouldn't feel any differently toward her. He knew without a doubt that she would do what she felt was in the best interest of all parties involved, and he couldn't ask for more than that.

Well, he could, but it wouldn't be right of him. She might be his little sister, he might have practically raised her, but it wasn't like he would bend her over his knee if she messed this up. The shrewd little she-were would never allow something so undignified. Just the thought of it had him fighting back his chuckles.

Unfortunately, he also realized that he was at a distinct disadvantage. While he knew every member on The Council and was friendly with most, it could actually hinder him in this situation. Probably they would want to rule in his favor, but he wondered how many would go against him, just to prove that they weren't playing favorites or letting loyalties influence their decisions.

"Why a challenge?" Cortez asked. "Have you tried proving your right to Mr. Braddock?"

"No, sir. I was not given the chance."

"Well, you have it now." Elder Cortez looked out over the room and right to Lynk. "Mr. Braddock, come forward if you will."

Lynk started shaking again, but there wasn't anything Kieran could do about it this time. "It's okay, baby. Just let him have his test, and then everyone will know that you don't belong to him. It's the fastest way to get this over with."

"Right. Okay. Sure. Got it," Lynk babbled, his head bobbing up and down like it was on springs as he eased past Kieran and shuffled toward the front of the meeting hall.

It took every sliver of willpower that Kieran possessed not to fly across the room, snatch Lynk up, and rip out Zasha's throat when Lynk stopped just beside the vampire. This was wrong. Lynk belonged to him, and everyone knew it. Why did they have to play these fucking games to prove it?

"State your name for the record," Torren said quietly. It was beyond obvious that he wasn't any more a fan of what was happening than Kieran. Still, they had to follow protocol, put on their shoes and tap dance so that everyone could see they were playing nice.

"Lynk Corrigan Braddock."

"Lynk, you understand that you are not allowed to use any form of magic to resist Mr. Gershwin's compulsion, correct?" Elder Layke Winters was probably the most softly spoken, benevolent man Kieran had ever met. Yet, there was something about him—an air of power and great wisdom that afforded him respect for nothing more than breathing.

"Yes, Layke...er, sir." Lynk bit his lip and blushed at the slip of the tongue. Kieran found it endearing. According to the smile on Elder Winters' face, he did as well.

"Okay, Mr. Gershwin, you may proceed."

Kieran's hands fisted on the top of his thighs, the short nails biting into his palms as he fought to remain in his seat when Zasha rested a hand on the side of Lynk's neck, right over Kieran's claiming mark. He could do this. He could get through this. It would all be over in a minute.

Zasha leaned forward, staring into Lynk's eyes, his lips only a breath away from Kieran's mate's. The tips of his fangs glistened in the overhead lights where they peeked out just below his upper lip.

Kieran sprang up out of his seat and growled viciously. "Stop!"

No one looked startled at his outburst. It was almost as if they had been expecting it. "Yes, Mr. Delaney?" his sister asked with a smirk on her painted lips.

Feeling less than stable and unable to shake it off, it took Kieran a while before he felt he could speak without snarling at her. "Does he have to touch him?"

"No, I suppose not," Elder Cortez answered instead. "Mr. Gershwin, you will refrain from touching Mr. Braddock throughout the remainder of this hearing."

Zasha didn't look happy about it, but he let his hand fall away, and Kieran finally felt a little more in control of himself. He refused to sit down, though. If Zasha broke his word, Kieran was ready. He'd be across the room and on top of the asshole before he could even blink.

"Kiss me," Zasha commanded Lynk, but loud enough for the whole room to hear him.

Lynk leaned away and snarled. It was a very human sound, but Kieran approved, and a satisfied rumble vibrated his chest.

Rubbing at the side of his neck, Zasha was actually grinning as he turned back to the elders. "I just needed to know his reaction without compulsion, so that I can tell if he's faking it or not." Then he refocused on Lynk, staring deep into his eyes.

Kieran knew the exact moment that it worked because his bond with Lynk faded until it was just barely a whisper between them. He didn't like it, didn't appreciate being disconnected from his mate, but he did realize that it proved one very vital point. Lynk was not Zasha's true mate.

"Undress," Zasha ordered.

In a trance, Lynk's fingers began fumbling with the buttons on his shirt. He looked straight ahead, though it was unclear if he was actually seeing anything. When he'd undone half of the buttons, though, Kieran had seen enough. "Lynk," he called. "Stop."

Lynk's fingers instantly stilled, though he didn't look around at him.

"Come here, now."

The entire audience watched as Lynk turned on his heels and glided across the room, moving quickly but gracefully until he stood directly in front of Kieran.

Cupping his lover's face in both hands, Kieran dipped his head and pressed their lips together, inhaling the sweet scent that was uniquely Lynk. "Snap out of it, sugar. You belong to me, not that idiot."

A little shudder worked its way through Lynk's body, he blinked several times, and then his eyebrows drew together in confusion. "How did I get back here? Did it work?"

"He's faking of course!" Zasha shouted. "They planned the entire thing! I demand a challenge."

"Enough!" To Kieran's surprise it was Leader Tuesday who spoke, rising from his seat in the front of the room and stepping forward to address the elders. "I apologize." He gave a little bow of respect. "I only supported Zasha because I believed his claim to be true. It is what a good leader does, and as someone who has lost his own mate, I did not want to see a member of my coven endure that. I can see now that Zasha is mistaken, and so was I."

"What?" Zasha gasped. "No! I can feel him. I can feel his soul tugging at mine."

"Perhaps we should conduct the rest of this meeting in private," Elder Camdin Maywater suggested in his musical voice.

"No." Leader Tuesday moved closer to the platform. "We have nothing to hide."

"We'll see about that," Kieran mumbled, taking Lynk's hand and marching to the front of the hall to stand beside Leader Tuesday. He'd had enough. He wanted answers, and if no one was going to ask the pertinent questions, then he sure as hell would. "Where is Thane Braddock?"

"Excuse me?" The coven leader appeared genuinely perplexed by the question. "Thane Braddock?"

Kieran gave Lynk a little nudge between the shoulders, offering support but encouraging him to speak up with what he knew. "My brother, Thane, is being held in a well on your lands. He's been there for several months now, being starved and fed from while he wastes away."

There was no shock, no contempt written in Tuesday's expression. There was, however, a cold, hard calculation that chilled Kieran's blood. Turning to the gatherers, Tuesday pointed one long, slim finger at his guards, Gideon and Axton. "You know the well?"

"Yes, sir," Gideon answered at once, while Axton simply dipped his head in agreement.

"I want you to check it out personally. Do not tell anyone else what you're doing or why you are going there. If you meet with resistance, back off and inform me immediately. Do you understand?"

One thing was for certain. Whether he was behind Thane's abduction or not, Leader October Tuesday—*what a ridiculous name*—was born to lead. Hell, even Kieran wanted to jump to attention and do as the man bid when he used that confident tone.

"Yes, sir," both guards answered in stereo before marching down the aisle between the bench seats and disappearing through the double doors at the back of the room.

Kieran wasn't completely convinced that it hadn't all been just for show, but the vampire's actions must have swayed Lynk in some way. "Thank you," he said with respect. Tuesday arched one sculpted eyebrow and bowed his head in acknowledgement. Then Lynk turned to Zasha. "I think there is something that you need to know."

"Does it have to do with why you are pretending that you cannot feel the connection between us?" Each word was forced through gritted teeth, and Zasha looked mad enough to spit nails.

"Yes, actually," Lynk answered, and Kieran could hear the smile in his voice. "I am not pretending anything, however. I do not feel a connection between us because one simply does not exist. Kieran is my mate—my destined mate."

Zasha growled and took a step forward, but his leader stopped him with a hand to his chest. "You will calm down and listen to what the boy has to say."

Lynk didn't look very happy about being referred to as a boy. He didn't comment, though, choosing instead to address Zasha with his next words. "Thane is my twin. We share an energy, which means our magic is twinned and more powerful when we're together. We can even speak telepathically if we're close enough to one another."

Maybe Zasha was still too angry to follow Lynk's train of thought to its conclusion, but Kieran could see the dawning enlightenment in Tuesday's eyes. Instead of interrupting, however, the vampire smiled reassuringly, encouraging Lynk to continue.

"I think you are feeling Thane's energy flowing from me. I don't know for sure, but I believe that is why you think I'm your mate while it is really Thane who you should be concentrating on."

"Thane?" The look on Zasha's face was priceless and almost comical. "The man you just said was being held captive in a well? He's been this close to me for months now?" Then his features darkened, his fangs elongated, and the veins around his eyes stood out in sharp relief against his pale skin. "Someone I trusted is hurting him, and that *someone* will pay for it."

Proving once again why he was leader of their coven, Tuesday didn't wait to be asked. He patted Zasha on the shoulder, giving him a little push toward the door. "Go get your mate, Zasha, but be smart about it. If you are blinded by your rage, you could do more damage than good."

Zasha appeared to calm a bit, and he jerked his head in what Kieran thought might have been understanding. "Thank you, sir."

"I should go with you."

Lynk had lost his goddamn mind if he thought that Kieran was going to allow him to go traipsing into enemy territory without him. "No, you're not."

"I need to do this, Kieran. If someone realizes what's going on and moves Thane, I'm the only one who can find him."

It was logical and practical, but Kieran still didn't like it. "Then I'm coming with you."

"I'll protect him," Zasha offered, earning him a glare and a snarl from Kieran. He did not need some bloodsucker protecting his mate.

"I'm going."

"You know I love you, but I can take care of myself, Kieran. I've got this." Lynk pushed up on his toes and kissed Kieran's lips. "Stay here and do what you can to help." His eyes flickered to Tuesday before coming back to settle on him. *"I can't be in two places at once without your help,"* he whispered into Kieran's mind.

He hated the very idea of Lynk being away from him. It went against every one of his natural instincts. In the end, he knew his mate was right. The fact that Lynk could turn everyone into toads with his magic went a long way in forming his decision as well. *"If you get into trouble, I want you to hide. I don't care if it hurts your pride or not. You hide and wait for me. Got it?"*

"Got it," Lynk whispered, giving him one last kiss. Then he was gone, disappearing through the back doors with Zasha.

"I'll go with them," Raith announced, rising to his feet. The witch had been somber and aloof since Halloween, but Kieran knew he'd do whatever was necessary to keep his brothers safe, so he offered a nod of thanks.

Raith returned his nod and hurried out of the meeting hall.

"Well, I guess we could have all saved a lot of time and trouble if we'd just listened to Kieran in the first place." Jory Lahman huffed and flopped back in his seat, looking very disgruntled.

"Why didn't you?" Leader Tuesday sounded mildly curious and nothing more.

"No offense," Torren began then stopped to clear his throat. "You are a very powerful man with an extremely large coven."

"Why would I be offended by such wonderful compliments?"

Kieran snorted out a laugh at the amusement dancing in Tuesday's honey-colored eyes. The man wasn't nearly as egotistical and ruthless as he'd been led to believe.

"Tober, don't be such an ass," Elder Cortez admonished around a chuckle. "You know these greenhorns. You practically had them pissing in their pants." The vampires shared a good laugh at this before sobering.

"*You* agreed with everything we said!" Jory accused, waving his finger in Cortez's face. "Why didn't you just go and ask him in the first place?" He leaned forward in his chair and pointed down the row of elders to Layke. "And you probably know him, too. You know everyone!"

Layke grinned crookedly. "Of course I know Tober. He's been a thorn in my side for years."

"Pain in the ass is more like it," Cortez grumbled.

Kieran was becoming more confused by the moment, and it didn't sit well with him. "What the hell is going on here?"

"Look." Cortez held both hands up in a placating gesture. "Layke and I have known Leader Tuesday for many years. But, so have Stavion and his Enforcers. Why are you not questioning their decision to draw him under suspicion?"

"Well—"

"I'll tell you why," Cortez interrupted, which was a good thing since Kieran had no idea what he'd planned to say. "We want to believe the best of people, but there is always the potential for evil. If there was even the slightest possibility that Tuesday had turned against us, then that needed to be taken very seriously."

"We cannot charge into a volatile situation against a powerful enemy without first thinking forward to the consequences," Layke added, sounded unusually serious.

"I find myself flattered." Turning to Kieran, Tuesday shrugged unconcernedly for someone who'd just been accused of a whole slew of wrongdoings. "They're correct, though. Not to blow my own horn, but Snake River is one of the largest in the country. If I had harbored ill will toward any of you, it would have taken an army to defeat me."

He talked a big game, and he certainly sounded convincing, but Kieran's suspicious nature wouldn't allow him to trust blindly. Until it was proven beyond a shadow of a doubt that Leader Tuesday was as innocent as he claimed to be, Kieran wasn't letting his guard down.

"Besides, I never said he was guilty." Leaning back in his seat, Cortez appeared the epitome of ease. "I just thought it was suspicious that he never filed sanction against Lynk for his little magic trick."

Leader Tuesday chuckled. "It did cross my mind, but fortunately, good sense won out. I understood that Mr. Braddock feared for not only his life but the safety of his companions. I can't fault a man for going to any measures to protect those he cares about, as it is what I would do myself."

The vampire spoke as though he was from a different time, and in some ways he was. Having roamed the earth for more than a thousand years, Tuesday had lived through all the changes the world and its societies had undergone. His speech and mannerisms were formal, reeking of class and sophistication. Maybe he'd chosen the social etiquettes of the time period he most loved and just stuck with it.

"Just out of curiosity, how did you know that your brother is being held in my coven?" he asked of Torren.

"Lynk felt his energy when we arrived the other day," Kieran hurried to say, not wanting anyone to give away too much information. "They can also communicate telepathically as Lynk said. They spoke in a dream earlier today." There. That answered the question without revealing too many of their secrets.

Glancing up at Torren, he noticed that the elder was staring down at him in gratitude and perhaps a bit of admiration. It was good to know that he wasn't the only one still skeptical.

"Thane said he'd been abducted in Belgium," Torren added quietly, but he was examining Tuesday carefully, seeming eager for his reaction.

Tuesday's demeanor became frigid, and a muscle in his jaw ticked as he ground his teeth together with such force that Kieran could actually hear it. It wasn't the response he'd expected, and he didn't know what it meant, either.

"How fast can you get us to Snake River?" he asked, looking directly into Kieran's eyes.

"How fast do I need to?"

"Five minutes ago. Zasha has family in Leuven, Belgium. He visits every year in the spring."

Chapter Fifteen

"Who are you calling?"

They'd just pulled up to the gates of Snake River when Zasha grabbed his cell phone from the dashboard of the SUV and began dialing. "Gideon. They should be at the well by now." He pressed the phone to his ear and waited.

Lynk fidgeted nervously in his seat, dividing his attention between Zasha and the view beyond the windshield. He really wanted to shut everything out and try to connect with Thane, but he wanted to know what Gideon and Axton had found first.

"He's not answering." Zasha frowned at the display screen as he came to a stop in front of the main house, the lights inside glowing brightly and welcoming. Then he shook himself and opened his door. "We'll take the ATVs from here."

"Where is the well?" Raith asked, sounding much more hostile than Lynk felt the situation warranted.

"I know the way. Just follow me."

"That's not what I asked."

"I don't have time to draw you a fucking map. Let's go!"

Lynk wasn't reassured by Zasha's evasiveness. It was a simple question that could have been answered just as easily. What was he hiding?

Jogging after the vampire, Lynk rounded the corner of the house just in time to hear Zasha curse. "The ATVs are gone. We're going to have to go on foot. It's not too far from here."

How convenient. Lynk didn't mind hoofing it, but it would take longer, which allowed more time for something to go wrong. He was starting to get a very bad vibe from Zasha as well, and it did nothing to calm his nerves.

As they started off across the side lawn toward the trees that surrounded the house, Lynk allowed Raith to lead him, taking the opportunity to try and contact Thane. Concentrating all of his energy and picturing Thane in his mind, he pushed with everything he had, hoping he could reach his brother.

In return, there was just a slight brush that made the hairs on his arms stand up, like the hum of a very low wattage of electricity. Either Thane was succumbing to his injuries and starvation, or he had been moved farther away.

"I can barely feel him," he whispered to Raith. Even as he spoke the words the connection grew fainter until it was more like a gentle breath tickling the back of his neck.

"How much farther?" Raith asked of their guide.

"Not far." Zasha was moving at a good pace now that they had come out on the other side of the trees into an open field. Without slowing, he pointed ahead of them to three vast windmills standing like sentinels in the moonlight. "The well is at the base of the center one."

Even from the distance and in the dim light, Lynk could tell that the area around the windmills was deserted. "Where are Gideon and Axton?"

Zasha shook his head but didn't answer, increasing his strides until Lynk was jogging to keep up with him. Climbing the slope that inclined toward the windmills, a sense of danger washed over Lynk, causing him to stumble and nearly fall on his face if Raith hadn't caught him.

"What is it?"

"He's not here." Instead of growing stronger as it should when he moved closer to the well, Thane's energy was nearly nonexistent now. There was another force inside the clearing, however—something malevolent, watching them, waiting for them. "Stop. We have to go back."

"We're already here," Zasha argued, charging over the crest of the hill in his determination to reach the windmills.

"We have to know for sure," Raith added grudgingly. "We need to at least see if there's any evidence that Thane was here at one time."

It was with a great deal of trepidation that Lynk approached the old stone well. Zasha was leaning over the edge of it, peering into the depths with a frown on his face. "Hello?" he called, his voice echoing back to him.

"Lynk!"

So intent on establishing the connection with Thane, Lynk had been inadvertently blocking out his mate. *"I'm here, Kieran. Something's not right. I don't think Thane is here."*

"Get out of there. Get away from Zasha now! Run as fast as you can and hide. I'm coming for you."

The fear and urgency in Kieran's voice propelled him into movement, but he'd taken only a half a dozen steps away from the well when a ragged moan drifted up from the bottom. "Thane!" Without thought, he sprinted forward, grabbed the edge of the stones, and leaned over as far as he dared. "Thane! Are you okay? Can you talk to me?"

He received only an agonized groan in response.

"We're going to get you out. Just be still." If they didn't get him out soon, it would be too late. Thane hovered just on the brink of death, his energy growing fainter with each passing second.

A loud grunt from behind him drew his attention, and Lynk started to turn to investigate. Sickening pain exploded in his temple, temporarily blinding him and sending him stumbling backward, right over the stone lip of the well and plunging into darkness.

Because of the awkward angle at which he'd fallen, the back of his head smacked against the unyielding wall, and everything went black.

* * * *

"Lynk? Lynk!" Kieran stomped down on the accelerator. "Lynk!" he yelled aloud, startling his passengers.

Leader Tuesday occupied the front passenger seat while all three of Kieran's brothers had crammed into the backseat of the extended cab pickup, resolute in helping in any way they could.

He was almost there. The lights that illuminated the main entrance bathed the road just a quarter mile in front of him. At the same time, he was too far away. His connection with Lynk hadn't been severed, but it was like getting static over a telephone line when he knew the other person was still there but only caught snatches of the conversation.

Barely tapping on the brake, he jerked the wheel hard, turning the truck onto the long drive and barreling right through the open gates. No one tried to stop him. "Why are the gates open?"

"I phoned ahead," Tuesday answered distractedly. His eyes were locked on the main house, and he reached up to point through the windshield. "That's Zasha's vehicle."

Tires screeching, the back of the pickup slid sideways as Kieran stomped on the brake and threw the transmission into park. He didn't even bother turning off the engine before flying out the driver's door and sprinting to the side of big brick house.

He had no idea where the well was located or where he was going, but he could still feel Lynk, so he followed that thin rope of recognition, allowed it to guide him, reel him in. His feet pounded over the uneven earth, crunching the dying grass beneath his boots. Charging into the tree line, he never slowed his pace even as he was forced to dodge low-hanging branches and leap over fallen logs.

When he burst out on the other side of the small forest, he finally stopped and waited for his comrades to catch up to him. "There." It wasn't a question as he pointed to the three enormous windmills rising up from the ground. His link to his mate was growing stronger, clearer. He could feel Lynk's panic as if it was his own, but he pushed it to the back of his mind, needing to concentrate if he hoped to rescue his lover.

"Just at the bottom of the middle one," Tuesday confirmed.

Kieran took off again, sprinting up the small incline and stripping out of his clothes as he went. Stopping once more when he'd reached the top of the slope, he kicked his boots off, shoved his jeans down his legs, and let the fury within him fuel his change. Once completely transformed, he tossed his head back and howled to the moon.

His enemy would know he was coming.

Zasha had taken his mate, the sunshine to his darkness and the very air that he breathed. Death was too lenient a punishment, but letting the bloodsucker live was out of the question.

More howls ripped through the night, followed by vicious growling as his brothers moved in to flank him on either side. It wasn't until that moment that Kieran realized there were four enormous beasts, two on each side of him.

So Leader Tuesday was a hybrid.

While the information was surprising and produced a whole slew of questions, it wasn't exactly pertinent at that very moment. Besides, it didn't affect him in any way. If anything, Kieran was happy to have extra muscle on his side. As he prowled toward his destination, Kieran's lupine eyes cut through the darkness, easily spotting the three slumped figures on the ground. All were much too large to be Lynk, however. So, where was he?

His advanced hearing picked up the crash of footsteps over branches in the trees behind him, but he ignored it. That would be Torren with reinforcements, but once Kieran got his hands on Zasha, he wouldn't be needing them.

* * * *

A soft groan puffed through his lips when Lynk finally came awake. He wished he could have kept right on sleeping. His head pounded, feeling much too large for the rest of his body. When he pried open his eyes, he was struck with the momentary sense of panic when he couldn't immediately see anything.

"Easy," a raspy voice answered his silent fear.

"Thane?" Oh, gods, even the sound of his own voice was going to split his skull in two. Trying to get his wits about him, Lynk only then realized that he was leaning against another body with a large arm wrapped around his chest to keep him from sliding under the frigid water that reached up to his navel.

"I'm here." Thane's voice was weak and hoarse, coming out as barely more than a frail whisper. "Are you okay?"

Getting his feet under him, Lynk eased out of his brother's hold, shivering when the icy water surged up to his shoulders by the time his feet found the bottom of the well. "I'm fine." His teeth clacked together and his muscles vibrated continuously, trying to warm his core body temperature. How had Thane survived for so long down here?

"Help will come."

Lynk had no reservations about that. Kieran had already been on his way before Lynk had blacked out, and he'd sounded furious. It was keeping him and Thane alive until his mate could reach them that worried him. How much time had passed since he'd fallen into the depths of the well? It couldn't have been long, but every second that passed, their hopes of survival dwindled with it.

"You said they feed on you. How do they get in?"

Thane took his hand in the darkness and pulled him to the other side of the well. The fingers wrapped around his palm were much too cold, too thin, and it made Lynk's heart hurt. He didn't have long to dwell on the injustice of what his brother had suffered, though. His arm was lifted, and his hand pressed flat against a plank of wood.

"What is this?"

"Door," Thane answered then fell into a coughing fit that wracked his entire body.

"Okay, shh." Lynk rubbed at Thane's back. "Just rest. I'm going to get us out of here."

The loud howling of one very pissed off werewolf erupted into the night, echoing down the well and bouncing off the stones until it was as though the beast was confined down there with them. The sound was terrifying, but it made Lynk smile. Then four other howls, each distinctly different from the other, rolled across the breeze, and Lynk's heart broke into a gallop as excitement overwhelmed him.

"My mate is here, and he's really unhappy."

* * * *

The unconscious men on the ground turned out to be Raith, Axton, and Gideon. Where was Lynk, though? And where the hell was Zasha?

"Kieran!"

The sound of his mate's voice hit him like a freight truck, and Kieran practically dove toward the well. *"Lynk? Are you okay? Are you hurt?"*

"I took a knock on the head, but I'm fine. Thane's not going to make it much longer, though. There's a door here that I think might lead to one of those windmills. I'm going to try to get through it."

"Where is Zasha?"

Lynk's voice came back inside his mind, cold and hard. *"I don't know, but when we find him, he's mine."*

"Not if I get to him first. I'm going to guess that door leads to the center windmill. Try to open the door now."

He heard a few muttered words and then a loud explosion that shook the ground beneath his feet. "Still got it," Lynk called up to him, proud and cocky.

"Can you see anything?" There was no answer, though. *"Lynk, talk to me, sugar. What do you see? What's going on?"* Still, he heard nothing.

Before he could get himself too worked up, though, there was another enormous boom. The door on the windmill fell from its hinges into a pile of rubble, and Lynk stood there, grinning from ear to ear. "Can I get some help?"

Parker was at his side in an instant, lifting a very thin and frail-looking man into his arms. Kieran barely noticed. His whole world had narrowed to his mate as Lynk sprinted toward him. Opening his arms, he caught the smaller man and crushed him close, rumbling in his chest as he nuzzled against Lynk's head, face, and neck.

"I'm fine, Kieran. A knot the size of Memphis on the back of my head, but otherwise, I'm okay."

"I'm so proud of you, sugar." Someone stepped up beside them, trying to remove Lynk from his arms, and Kieran snapped at the intruder, snarling viciously.

"Shut up," Torren chastised him. "I just want to see that my brother is okay."

"I'm fine, Torren." Lynk pointed toward the windmill. "Thane is the one who needs help, and fast. Besides, I think you need to back off before Kieran eats you."

Yes, he did. While Kieran understood that bond between brothers, Lynk was his mate, and he wasn't about to release his hold on him when he'd just found him safe and mostly unmarred.

With the addition of Torren, Raven, Bannon, and the eldest Murphy brother, Devlin, there were now eight men milling about the small clearing. And that wasn't even including the three unconscious bodies on the ground, Lynk, or himself. Haven really was like one immense family. If someone messed with one of them, the entire coven came together with hostile intent.

"Give me the book!"

Kieran whirled around, Lynk still held protectively in his arms, and curled his lip at the sight before him. Axton was on his feet, his eyes wide and crazed as he clutched Raven to him, a gold blade resting against the vampire's throat.

"Where is Zasha?" Leader Tuesday countered, having reverted back to his usual form.

"Tell me where the book is!" The blade pressed more insistently at Raven's flesh, and the Enforcer flinched as though it burned him. Maybe it did. Gold was highly toxic and often lethal to vampires.

"Who are you working with?" Torren growled, advancing toward Axton. "Why do you want the book?"

"The circle will reward me if I deliver the book to them. They gave me the witch, led me to where he was hiding, and trusted me to watch over him. I have to produce the book now." Axton removed the dagger from Raven's neck and waved it around wildly. "Tell me where it is!"

"Who led you to the witch? When?" Leader Tuesday spoke with an air of calm authority, even though he was facing down a deranged vampire with a gold blade—not to mention the little fact that the coven leader was butt naked in the cold November wind.

"The circle!" Axton screamed. "They found me when I went home with Zasha. They gave me the key." He pointed at Thane to indicate which key he meant. "They come and harvest his blood. They're almost ready, but they need the book. I have to give them the book if I want the power they can give me."

Kieran really hoped he'd be the one that got to break the news to the idiot that it didn't matter if he handed over the Book of the Banished or not. He'd be long dead before the witches could ever "reward" him.

"Zasha has been a good friend to you." Tuesday clasped his hands in front of him and tilted his head to the side. "His family welcomed you into their home. What have you done to him, Axton?"

"He's alive."

"Where?"

"I'm not stupid," Axton spat. "If I tell you, then I have no leverage. You need me or you'll never find him. Now, give me the fucking book!"

Lynk wiggled out of Kieran's arms and crossed his arms over his chest. "I know where Zasha is."

Kieran wasn't sure if his mate was bluffing, but he sounded convincing. Apparently Axton agreed, because his eyes went even wider, and he lunged forward to grab Lynk by the upper arm. "Give me the book or I'll gut him like a fish." The stupid bloodsucker looked right at Kieran as he spoke, taunting him, goading him.

As the haze of murderous fury descended over him, Kieran's mind went completely blank and his beast took over, demanding vengeance. The next few seconds passed in a blur of growling, biting, ripping, and clawing at any part of Axton he could reach. When Kieran finally returned to his senses, he had Lynk in his arms once more, and Axton was splayed on the ground, his sightless eyes staring up at the moon as blood pooled in the grass beneath his lifeless body.

Lynk looked a little green around the gills, and he was shaking as he clung to Kieran. So, when he finally spoke, his words were so unexpected that Kieran actually chuffed in laughter.

"Well, good thing that I really *do* know where Zasha is."

* * * *

Lynk hadn't personally known where Zasha was, but Thane did. Though they hadn't been bonded, their connection was still there, allowing Thane to feel his mate's presence. They'd speculated on it quite a bit, but it was kind of liberating to know that he'd been correct in his assumption as to why Zasha had been so obsessed with him.

It hadn't taken long to find the vampire beneath a trapdoor in the far left windmill. He'd been drugged and bound, but was a little groggy on the details of how exactly Axton had gotten the drop on him. While Zasha's behavior had seemed suspicious when he'd led them to the well, he really had just been worried for Thane and in a rush to get to him. Lynk could understand that single-minded pursuit when it came to the safety of the people who mattered most to him.

Raith was spitting mad, snarling and bitching about Axton drugging him as well. Once he'd learned that the asshole vampire had been the one to push Lynk into the well—as well as the horrors of what he'd put Thane through—Lynk imagined Axton should be glad he was already dead. What Kieran had done to him would probably seem like child's play compared to Raith's fury.

It really hadn't been a very well thought out or executed plan. Clearly, Axton hadn't been very bright, rest his soul. Part of Lynk mourned the loss of life, but the rational part of him understood that it couldn't have been avoided. Even if Axton hadn't died at Kieran's hands, The Council would have ordered his execution almost immediately.

He just wished there had to been time for them to discover the name of the circle of witches he had been working with. On the other hand, he supposed they had enough clues to lead them in the right direction. It had to be a local coven, one with ties in Belgium.

There was also the strong likelihood that it was the same group that had attacked them on Halloween. It wouldn't exactly be easy to identify them, but Lynk had confidence that they'd find them eventually.

There would be more as well. All over the world, covens, packs, circles, and all types of paranormals were searching out the Braddocks, desperate to have a key to the Book of the Banished. For now, however, the book was safe, and Lynk and his brothers had survived once again. They'd found one of their missing brethren, their family was slowly being reunited, and Lynk had his *Infinity*.

As things went, he figured he was a pretty lucky guy.

Chapter Sixteen

"I want to see my mate," Zasha demanded.

"No," Torren countered. "I have some questions for you, plus Thane is in no condition to be getting worked up right now."

Lynk was having a hard time picking a side on this one. While he wanted some answers and certainly wanted to protect his brother, he'd be a snarling, spitting mess if someone tried to keep him away from Kieran.

"I'll answer your questions." Zasha slumped back against the cushions of the sofa where they all gathered in the living room of the house Lynk shared with his brothers and mate. "I'm not going to hurt him. I just need to see him."

The vampire sounded drained, but he'd refused to leave Thane. So while Leader Tuesday cleaned up the mess in his coven, Zasha had traveled back to Casper with them. No one would let him near Thane, though, and Lynk felt a little guilty about that. Still, Torren said it was for the best until Thane could recover from his ordeal, and for once, Lynk agreed.

Thane was barely more than skin and bones, covered in bruises, bite marks, cuts, and angry-looking sores. It was a miracle that he was even still alive after what he'd endured.

"How did Axton get Thane into the country?" Torren asked, leaning forward in his chair and clasping his hands together between his knees as he stared at Zasha unblinkingly.

"I don't think he did." There was a moment of silence while Zasha apparently tried to gather his thoughts. "Axton doesn't have any family, and he never really fit in at Snake River. I guess I felt sorry for him." He sighed heavily, but kept his head up and his shoulders back. "I always go home to Belgium to visit my family in the spring. A few years ago, I asked Axton to come with me."

"You asked him? Not the other way around?"

Lynk didn't know why the distinction was important, but he trusted Torren to get the information they needed.

"Yes." Zasha bobbed his head. "It was just after he'd come to our coven, and he was still having problems making friends and settling in. I thought it would do him some good to get away for a while. That was the first time I took him with me. It just kind of became an annual thing after that."

"How did he meet these witches in Belgium?" Shifting around in his recliner, Kieran spread his thighs and held out a hand for Lynk to come to him while he spoke to Zasha.

Uncaring of what any of the men in the room thought, Lynk rose from the floor and settled into his mate's lap. Curling into the man's much larger body, Lynk rested his head on Kieran's shoulder, sighing happily when those big, muscled arms wrapped around him protectively.

Clearly his lover still had reservations about Zasha. Since the idiot had gone as far as to bite him, Lynk really couldn't blame Kieran for his distrust. The vampire was Thane's *Infinity*, though, and therefore family. Sooner or later, Kieran was going to have to get over his dislike of the man.

"Axton said he wanted to give me some time alone with my family, and that he was going to go explore the city. He'd been coming home with me for five or six years by that point, so he knew the area well. It was pretty common by that point for him to go out on his own while we were there, so I didn't think anything of it, either. I'm guessing that's when he met the witches."

"You think that circle is responsible for getting Thane back to the States." Lynk bobbed his head, frowning in concentration while he tried to follow the path of logic. "That makes sense, but where were they keeping him? Thane said he was held captive for nearly two years, but only the last few months were spent in that well."

"I can't answer that." His upper lip curled, and Zasha looked royally pissed off. "I promise that I'll find out, though." He looked right into Torren's eyes and growled. "I'll make them pay for what they did to him."

"Maybe Thane can tell us more when he wakes up," Lynk hurried to add, trying to defuse the hostility flashing in the vampire's eyes. "I don't think it's a huge stretch to assume the witches who attacked us on Halloween could be involved with this. I think we need to find out what they know."

Torren dipped his head in Lynk's direction. "I agree. We have Thane with us, and once he's stronger, we can focus on getting Mikko back as well. How he came to be in that well is important, though. We have to make sure it doesn't happen to anyone else."

"Speaking of that happening to other people"—Kieran sat up a little straighter, repositioning Lynk in his lap—"we started looking for Thane in Snake River because Aslan said he was held as a blood slave in a coven nearby. Snake River is the only one in the vicinity." He said no more after that, but the accusation was clear in his voice.

"We're not the only coven." His eyebrows drew together, and Zasha shook his head once. "There's another coven that lives near the base of the mountains not too far from here. It's a small coven, only ten or twelve members."

"How do you know that?" Torren looked disgruntled as he rubbed at the back of his neck. "Why didn't I know that?"

Zasha shrugged. "Like I said, they're small and mostly keep to themselves. Axton lived with them before coming to Snake River."

Alarm bells went off in Lynk's head, and he sat up so quickly that the top of his head whacked against Kieran's chin. He barely felt it, though. "Near the mountains, away from heavily populated areas, it sounds like the perfect place if someone needed to hide something."

"Or someone," Zasha growled. "You think Axton kept Thane there." He growled again but bobbed his head in agreement. "You're right. It makes sense, and everything is too connected to be mere coincidence."

"Can you show us where this coven is?"

Coming out of his thoughts, Zasha lifted his head to face Torren again and nodded. "I know the general area."

"I think everyone needs to rest tonight, but we'll call another meeting tomorrow to go over the situation and plan a course of attack." Torren seemed much less volatile now that they had a plan. "You're welcome to spend the day here, but Thane needs to rest now."

"I just want to see him." There was pain in Zasha's amber eyes, and he sounded so sad. "I won't disturb him, but I need to see that he's okay. Please?"

"Torren," Lynk said softly, his eyes pleading for his brother to stop being such a control freak for once in his life.

With a heavy sigh, Torren pushed up from his chair and motioned for Zasha to come with him. "Follow me, and I'll show you where he's sleeping."

"Thank you," Zasha whispered to Lynk before turning his gaze to Kieran. "I know you probably hate me, and I can't blame you, but I am so sorry for what I put you through."

To Lynk's complete surprise, Kieran offered his hand to the vampire. "I get it. I'd do whatever it took to get my mate back if I thought someone was keeping him from me."

"That was nice of you," Lynk whispered up to his mate once they were alone in the room. "I think he's a good guy. I'm glad you're willing to give him a chance."

Kieran huffed and kissed the top of his head. "Yeah, well, let's not break out the friendship bracelets just yet. I won't kill him, but that's all I'm promising right now."

Ducking his head to hide his smile, Lynk knew it was a big step for Kieran. Considering his possessive attitude and anger management issues, not murdering the vampire was a pretty good place to start.

* * * *

"I'm coming for you, Lynk."
"I'm counting on it," his lover called back from the distance.
Kieran could hear the smirk in his mate's voice, practically feel the anticipation flowing off of him. It was a game they often played on warm summer nights, one he always looked forward to. The moon lit his path, their bond pulled him deeper into the forest, and every part of Kieran thrummed with the desire to get his hands on his mate.

He knew from experience he'd find Lynk within the woods, gloriously naked, and spread out for him like a feast for a king. Closer, closer, he was almost there. His mouth watered, his dick ached, and need gripped him in a vice hold.

Shaking himself out of his memory, Kieran smiled inwardly as he stalked his prey. So many times they'd played this game in their previous lives, but it never got old or boring. This time, however, he had the added advantage of his werewolf senses to help guide him through the night.

He'd been reluctant at first when Lynk had suggested it, but as always, his little mate had worn him down. It helped that they were on Haven lands, and Kieran knew there were Enforcers patrolling the grounds, always watchful for any danger. Still, he'd feel much better when he reached Lynk. The man was crafty, doubling back several times to try and throw Kieran off his scent, but Kieran wouldn't be distracted. The prize was too great, and he aimed to win it.

Still, he stalked slowly through the trees, allowing the need and desire to grow inside them both, prolonging the exquisite torture until they were reunited once more.

There had been a flurry of activity in the weeks since Axton's untimely demise, and Kieran found himself in meetings more times than not. They still hadn't located the coven near the mountains, but there were signs to indicate that they were getting closer.

Unfortunately, it didn't leave a lot of free time to heat up the sheets with his mate. Kieran hated it, but on the bright side, it only made it that much more explosive when they finally found their way together.

Pushing aside a leafless branch, Kieran growled in satisfaction when he stepped into a very small clearing, just big enough for a blanket to be spread over the cold ground. His mate sprawled over the soft fleece on his back, his knees pulled back to his chest, clearly displaying the silicone toy pressed between his ass cheeks.

"What took you so long? I thought I was going to have to finish without you."

Game over. Kieran pounced, diving across the space between them and covering his lover in one swift move. The fur that covered his body blanketed Lynk, hopefully warming him as Kieran licked and nuzzled at the sweet-smelling flesh along the column of Lynk's throat.

Careful of his claws, he mapped every contour of his mate's body, memorizing each dip, curve, and indention. While parts of him were more beast than man, his cock and his mind were very much human, and both demanded Lynk's submission.

With each passing second, Kieran's need grew, swelling inside him until it shattered the last remaining remnants of his self-control. Gripping the base of the butt plug, he pumped it twice, hard and fast into Lynk's hole before wrenching it free.

His little man cried out, his back bowed, and that beautiful look of pleasure-pain that Kieran adored lit his handsome face. "Please, sir. Please."

Kieran had been slowly learning the ins and outs of Lynk's need to be dominated and why he so desperately craved it. Mostly, he didn't mind taking the reins in the bedroom, but he refused to hurt his mate. Thankfully, Lynk never asked it of him as he'd done in that life so many years ago.

It was just that Lynk's mind was always working, always thinking three steps ahead of everyone else. Sometimes, he needed Kieran to take over, help him clear the clutter from his brain, and let him simply exist for that small space of time. This, however, was not one of those times. Not for Kieran anyway. Here and now, they were not Master and slave, Dom and sub, or anything besides mates and equals.

"Kieran. You will call me Kieran."

"Yes, Kieran. Please. I need you. I'm so close already."

The soft pleading was music to his ears. Kieran looped his arm under Lynk's knee and spread him wide as he lined up the engorged crown of his cock with his lover's fluttering hole. Their bodies and souls were so in tune with each other that he immediately felt the ring of muscle relax for him, opening to allow him to plunge inside Lynk's channel, encasing himself to the base.

They both groaned at the invasion, though Kieran's was more of a strangled growl. Hard and fast, he rode his mate with brutal intensity, delighted when Lynk clutched at him and demanded more.

Kieran's orgasm barreled down on him, and there was no way to stop it. The full moon heightened his senses, making everything much clearer, crisper, and the feel of Lynk's velvet-lined channel massaging his throbbing cock was too much for him to withstand.

Just when he couldn't fight it any longer, Lynk began to chant words that Kieran didn't understand, but he found the litany beautiful none the less. When he'd finished, Lynk tilted his head to the side in perfect surrender, baring his throat to Kieran. His slender fingers wrapped around the back of Kieran's neck and urged him down. "Claim me, Kieran."

Something was building inside of him that had nothing to do with his impending climax. Kieran had a feeling that it was directly related to the words his lover had just spoken, but he couldn't make his brain work correctly to work through what it meant.

Going on instinct, he increased his pace, slamming even harder into Lynk's yielding body as he sank his canines through the supple flesh at the crook of his lover's neck. The tantalizing rush of blood over his tongue made his head spin, his balls draw tight, and his dick swell inside Lynk's snug passage.

Then bright lights burst inside his vision, his heart pounded wildly, and his body heated until he felt his very blood was boiling. A splash of liquid heat coated his belly, accompanied by the loud screams pouring from Lynk's plump lips as he tumbled over the edge and into orgasmic bliss.

Still disoriented from the intense emotions coursing through him, Kieran's release caught him by surprise, slamming into him and rolling him under a tide of unimaginable pleasure until he wasn't sure he'd survive it.

When he finally floated back down to earth, he found himself on his back with Lynk draped over him like a living blanket. *"I love you, sugar."*

"And I love you back, Kieran. I'm so lucky to have found you again."

Kieran knew the truth, though. He was the lucky one. Even though he'd fucked things up in his last go-round, fate had deemed him worthy of a second chance. He wouldn't take it for granted, either, cherishing it each and every day as the gift that it was. As the gift that Lynk was.

Their life together wouldn't always be sunshine and daisies. They'd fight. Kieran would probably find himself in the doghouse on more than a few occasions. More people would be coming for Lynk, and none of them would come with friendly intentions.

There was also the matter of finding the man who had sired his nephews. While part of him just wanted to sweep the whole thing under the rug and forget about it, he knew none of them would rest easy until they had some answers. He also knew that meant he was going to have to suck it up and contact Alpha Taylor of the Cloud Peak Pack to help him. It could wait for another day, though.

In that one special moment with Lynk, beneath the moon and stars, surrounded by the forest and cocooned together—right at that very second—Kieran's universe was flawless.

THE END

WWW.GABRIELLEEVANS.COM

ABOUT THE AUTHOR

Gabrielle Evans grew up in a small town in southern Oklahoma. We are talking one red light that may or may not work depending on the day of the week. She married her high school sweetheart and the rest is pretty much history. They have two very active boys and one high-strung wiener dog that keeps her constantly on the go. For now, she parks her car in central Indiana, but who knows what tomorrow will bring.

Gabrielle believes in love at first sight, falling hard and fast, taking chances, and grabbing your happy-ever-after with both hands. Most importantly, she believes that a great cup of coffee can cure anything.

Also by Gabrielle Evans

Everlasting Classic ManLove: Haven 1:
Caution: Contents Under Pressure
Everlasting Classic ManLove: Haven 2: *Faith, Trust, and Stardust*
Everlasting Classic ManLove: Haven 3: *Forgotten Sins*
Everlasting Classic ManLove: Haven 4: *Back Roads*
Everlasting Classic ManLove: Haven 5: *Invincible*

For all other titles, please visit
www.bookstrand.com/gabrielle-evans

Siren Publishing, Inc.
www.SirenPublishing.com

Lightning Source UK Ltd.
Milton Keynes UK
UKOW041840240712

196496UK00009B/80/P